A
CERTAIN
ENCHANTMENT

A CERTAIN ENCHANTMENT

•

MARILYN PRATHER

AVALON BOOKS
THOMAS BOUREGY AND COMPANY, INC.
401 LAFAYETTE STREET
NEW YORK, NEW YORK 10003

PRINTED IN THE UNITED STATES OF AMERICA
ON ACID-FREE PAPER
BY HADDON CRAFTSMEN, SCRANTON, PENNSYLVANIA

To Barbara Coleing
and
Pat Landrum
and
Rod, Bert & Rodney Rodriquez
and
Phil and Rhonda Stine—

for your gift of friendship

Chapter One

"**I**s there anything else I can do for you?"

Alison Hughes regarded the plump, balding man who stood behind the rental car counter. "There is one thing. Can you tell me how to get to Cortez Court?"

The agent gave her a brief smile. "Sure. No problem." He bent down behind the counter and came up with what appeared to be a brochure.

He unfolded it and Alison saw that it was a map. She watched as he showed her the way, highlighting with a yellow marker as he went. When he finished, the agent handed the map to her along with the keys to her newly leased Taurus. Something written across the top of the map caught Alison's eye. *Welcome to the Land of Enchantment,* it said.

She frowned. *Enchantment* was hardly the word she would use to describe this barren-looking place where dirt and dust seemed to have overtaken the grass, and even the trees appeared more brown than green.

"I hope you enjoy your stay here," the man said.

"Thank you," she responded with a forced smile.

After her luggage was loaded, Alison slipped behind the wheel of the red car. She took a moment to study the map more closely. The route looked easy enough to follow. But as she eased the Taurus out into the heavy traffic on the street, she was again plagued by the sense of disappointment that she'd felt on the shuttle bus from Santa Fe. Doubts about the wisdom of choosing a small, obscure town in a remote region of northern New Mexico crept into her mind.

"Cheer up," she admonished herself. The images that filled her head made it impossible for her to obey her own advice. Through the bus's grimy windows she had seen a stark landscape unfold, though the sky above it, as best she could tell, was a brilliant blue. Most of the region had appeared to be uninhabited, given over to sagebrush and stubby, twisted trees. But as she'd gotten closer to Taos, she'd noticed there were small orchards and low ramshackle houses that looked as if they were fashioned of mud. Now she remembered those austere little houses and wondered about the people who lived in them. Were they happy there, tending their apple and cherry trees?

The traffic in front of Alison ground to a halt at a stoplight. Distracted from her thoughts, she maneuvered into the lane where she needed to make her turn. She took advantage of the interlude to glimpse her face in the vanity mirror. What she saw added to her glumness. All of her lipstick and most of her blush had worn off. Today, even her eyes looked faded. The only bright thing about her was her strawberry blond hair and it could use a good combing.

Alison took a tube of lipstick and her comb from her purse. She managed to apply the color to her lips and smooth her hair into some semblance of order. Then the light blinked green. She made the turn and found she was on a one-way street. The street skirted a plaza. Alison surmised the area was downtown Taos.

Most of the buildings were plain and of adobe construction. But the several flags that flew above the buildings added a touch of cheerfulness to the scene. Traffic was slow and, as she passed, Alison took note of the galleries lining the street. Her colleagues at the Institute had been right when they'd said that Taos was an artists' mecca. That fact, too, made her question whether she would regret having selected Taos on impulse after learning she'd won the Deaver Foundation Grant. Especially when her friend and mentor, Paul, had suggested she might do well to consider the Green Mountains of New Hampshire instead. She hadn't had the courage to tell him that Taos sounded appealing to her for reasons having nothing to do with art, that it sounded like the kind of place where she could distance herself from certain bitter memories—memories of Erik, to be specific.

Brash and confident and terribly attractive, Erik VanMer had in the span of one evening captured her heart. And, in a matter of months, broken it.

Alison caught herself gripping the steering wheel. ''Relax,'' she muttered under her breath. Why had her thoughts taken such a negative bent? She was over Erik, wasn't she? Yes, and she'd learned a few lessons too.

She had come to realize what was important to her, that it was her career and the fulfillment she would find as she gained recognition as an artist. To let herself get discouraged now because she felt a little letdown over the scenery would only serve to stifle her creativity, and she couldn't afford for that to happen.

Alison wanted to believe that, by the time she returned to Cincinnati, she would have gained valuable experience—and, if she was really productive, a dozen or so paintings. She would need them. Just before she'd left, Paul had taken her aside and extended an invitation to be guest artist in his spring exhibition. The prospect was enough to unnerve her, but she was excited too. The show would bring in patrons from as far as Cleveland and Pittsburgh and would give her the exposure she must have to become a known artist.

Alison made the final turn into Cortez Court. She discovered the street was a cul-de-sac with, at most, eight houses on it. The neighborhood, located a number of blocks from downtown, was obviously an older one. For the first time since she'd landed at the airport in Santa Fe, she was reminded of home. The yards on Cortez Court were green and well groomed, and there were large oak trees lining the sidewalks. But despite the cozy atmosphere, Alison discovered there was a problem. None of the houses seemed to have numbers on them. Nor were there any mailboxes along the curb to tell her which house was 140 and belonged to Domingo and Rachel Ramirez, the couple from whom she was renting a loft.

Halfway around the cul-de-sac, she saw a man digging in a flower bed in the yard of one of the homes. Alison pulled up to the curb and put her car in park.

As she got out, she noticed that the man had stopped what he was doing and was heading her way. He had a hoe in his hand and, when he got nearer, she saw that he was young, perhaps not much older than herself. He wore a blue T-shirt and jeans, and he was good-looking. Extremely good-looking.

"I'm sorry to bother you," she said as he came up to her, "but can you tell me where one-forty is? I can't seem to locate any numbers on the houses," she added, hoping she didn't come across as dense.

He grinned at her as he leaned an elbow on the hoe. "That's because they're all hidden by bushes or vines. But you picked the right place anyway. This is one-forty." He gestured toward a vast weathered house that lay beyond the expanse of lawn where he stood.

Alison felt confused. She was certain from her phone conversations with Rachel Ramirez that Domingo was an older man. Rachel had said her husband was retired. Was this man Domingo and Rachel's son? He had dark wavy hair and eyes that were a warm shade of brown. He had a healthy tan too, yet he didn't look as if he were of Hispanic origin. All of a sudden, Alison realized that she was staring at him and she felt slightly flustered.

But he was staring at her as well, his mouth curved up in an easy smile. He seemed amused by her and that irritated her. She drew herself up straight. "Mr. Ramirez," she said, "I'm Alison Hughes."

His smile widened. "I figured that." He shifted the hoe to his other hand and wrapped his fingers around it. "I'm afraid I'm not Domingo Ramirez, though. My name's David Grier," he went on. "Rachel and Domingo were called away to Mexico City. Her brother was in a serious accident and they've gone to help his family."

That took Alison aback. "Oh. I'm . . . very sorry to hear that."

David Grier nodded. "He should be all right, but it's likely Rachel and Domingo will have to stay for a while." He paused, giving Alison an appraising look. "I'm afraid that in the meantime you'll have to put up with me as your landlord."

"I see." Alison wasn't sure how she felt about that. She wondered whether David was a neighbor of the Ramirezes. Maybe he and his wife lived next door—if he had a wife.

"Why don't we go inside and I can show you your room," David said. Then he paused, eyeing her car. "I assume you've got some luggage with you."

Alison saw what his intention was. "I can manage my suitcases."

David shot her another amused smile. "I'm sure you can, but consider it a service of the house. If you were staying in a hotel, a concierge would take your bags."

Another small tingle of annoyance went through Alison. She hoped that after today she and David Grier would have little cause to see each other. But he had a point on the matter of the luggage. "Okay. My things are in the trunk." She handed him the key and watched as he retrieved two of her cases, hefting them in his lean, brown arms.

"Follow me," he said over his shoulder.

They went up the walk to the door and he motioned for Alison to go ahead of him. She entered a marble-tiled foyer. There was a stairway to the left of the foyer. David put down one of the cases just long enough to close the door. "The loft's on the third floor," he explained as he lifted the suitcases again and started to mount the steps.

Alison went after him, only to find herself gulping for breath before she reached the top of the first flight. Would David find that funny too?

He paused on the landing above her, regarding her with a slight frown. "You'll have to take it slow," he cautioned. "Taos may be at the foot of some pretty tall mountains, but we're still at seven thousand feet altitude. It'll take your body a few days to adjust to the thinner air."

So that was the reason for her huffing and puffing. "Okay, thanks," she said as she struggled for breath. If she could talk, she would tell him that in Ohio she often hiked up steep Laurel Gorge with no effort at all.

David set down his load. "This happens to everyone when they first come to the land of *Poco Tiempo*," he said matter-of-factly.

"*Poco Tiempo?*" Alison took in another draft of air. "I thought this was the Land of Enchantment."

He chuckled. "It's that too. But *Poco Tiempo*, which kind of means slow time, is a local expression. In the smaller villages, we like to take things a lot slower than most Americans do. It's been our way of life. I guess some people could interpret *Poco Tiempo* as laziness." His eyebrows rose as if he wondered if she felt that way about the native philosophy.

"*Poco Tiempo* sounds good to me," she muttered, more to herself than to him. *Better than Land of Enchantment,* she was tempted to add, but didn't. "I believe the shuttle driver who brought us from Santa Fe to Taos could learn a thing or two about slow time."

"He must have been from Texas," David quipped.

Alison grinned. "Or Ohio." She realized her breathing had returned to normal. "I think I'm ready to tackle the next flight."

With another short rest, she made it to the loft. David stepped aside and motioned for her to go in ahead of him.

Alison's first glimpse of the loft was of a pleasing but small room. A closer look confirmed her impression. Sunlight streamed through the room's one window, spilling across the carpeted floor. The decor was strictly Southwestern, and there wasn't much furniture other than a quaint-looking canopied bed and a carved chest of drawers. Still, the room struck Alison as cozy.

David set her suitcases near the chest of drawers. "What do you think?" He came to stand beside her.

His nearness distracted her and, for a moment, she couldn't reply. "The loft's nice," she said, tilting her head back to look up at David.

"I'm glad you like it." David's eyes held hers for an instant before he turned away. "I'll get the rest of your cases."

Alison watched him go. She wished she didn't find David Grier so attractive. If he was around much, he could prove to be just the sort of distraction she was determined to avoid during her stay in Taos.

With determination, she turned her attention to a study of the loft. She decided the closet was just large enough to hold the clothes she had brought with her. And when she sat on it, the bed tested out comfortably, even if it sagged in the middle.

She next inspected the tiny bathroom off the loft. It contained a toilet, shower, and sink, adequate for her needs. But as she surveyed the room again, Alison saw there was a problem. Where would she be able to set up her easel and store her art supplies? The loft was to serve as her studio as well as her bedroom.

Debating the matter, her eyes focused on two framed pictures on the far wall. She went over for a closer look. They were mountain scenes, done in oil. Though colorful, they were obviously the work of an amateur.

"That's not the best view," a masculine voice said.

Alison turned to find David lugging her two other large suitcases and small travel case. He deposited them on the bed with a groan.

Embarrassed, Alison realized that one bag held her supplies. No wonder he had a problem carrying it.

David threw her a puzzled glance. "What do you have in there? Rocks? Are you a lapidary?"

She felt a familiar flash of anger, more than mere irritation. How fast her defenses rose when she thought she was being put down! Erik had done it countless times under the guise of a "joke." But she detected none of that familiar sarcasm in David's voice and her anger fled as quickly as it had risen.

David was watching her. Did he see the conflicting emotions that flared briefly inside her? If he did, he wasn't letting on.

"No, David," she replied at last. "I'm not a rock hound nor a geologist. But you could say that my equipment is in there."

"Is that so?" He appeared interested.

How could she keep him in suspense? Taking the key ring from her purse, she gave it to him, indicating the key that would open the large suitcase.

David said nothing for a moment, just hunkered down beside the case and peered inside. "So, you're an artist," he said finally. He picked up a tube of paint and one of the sable brushes from the case. Then he looked up at Alison. "There are quite a few artists in this town."

"Yes, I've heard." She watched as David's fingers ruffled the pliant bristles of the brush. "You mentioned a view, David."

He put the brush and paint away and got up. "Right over there." He pointed across the room. "Let me show you."

He led her to a pair of floor-to-ceiling draperies. Funny she hadn't taken note of them on her inspection of the room. He pushed the drapes back and, to her surprise, there were glass-paned double doors behind them. She saw a tiny balcony beyond the doors.

"Come outside," David invited.

Alison stepped out and found that the view was lovely. Through the trees, she spotted a small building. "What's that?" she asked.

"My *casa*."

She looked at David. "*Casa?* Isn't that the Spanish word for house?"

"Yes."

"So you live here then . . . I mean, with Domingo and Rachel?" Why was she stammering?

"That's right." He leaned against the iron railing that went around the balcony and gazed toward his home. But soon his eyes came back to Alison. "I moved into the *casa* a couple of years ago. Domingo and Rachel's son Martin and I grew up together. I've been a friend of the family for a long time."

It appeared that David didn't have a wife, after all. "I hope you don't mind my asking, but why do you call your home a *casa* instead of just a house?"

David grinned. "I don't mind you asking, and the reason it's called a *casa* is because that's what Domingo and Rachel have always called it. They built the *casa* as a guest house. For quite a while, they rented it out to vacationers and skiers. Now they're renting it to me.''

"Sounds like a good arrangement for all of you."

"It is."

They fell silent for a moment, and Alison's eyes were drawn again to David's hands. This time, they were curved around the railing. She thought they looked strong and capable and warm, and she wondered why she was intrigued by them. Maybe it was because she remembered that Erik's hands were thin, the fingers pale and tapered, almost like a woman's, and cool to the touch. She made herself look away, but David brought her attention back to him.

"There are a couple of other things I'd like to show you. That is, if you're not too anxious to start unpacking."

She couldn't very well refuse. "Not that anxious."

"Let's go then."

They went inside, and David led her back down the two flights of steps. They entered a long hallway and walked the length of it, past several closed doors. David stopped in front of the last door. He opened it and motioned for Alison to go first.

Alison stepped into a room that was small and bare except for a counter and two tiers of shelves that ran along one wall and a cabinet that stood in a corner.

"This used to be Rachel's utility room," David said. "Then, for a while, it was a studio for an aspiring jazz quartet." He crossed one leg in front of the other as he leaned against the wall.

"That's interesting," she said, though it wasn't particularly. She wondered why David had brought her here. Did he think he might entertain her by revealing a bit of the old house's history? When she saw that he was watching her, Alison began to pace.

"After the jazz quartet folded," he continued when she ended her pacing, "Rachel set up a greenhouse."

"I don't see any plants."

"An astute observation." He grinned, closing the distance between them. There seemed no escaping him. "The greenhouse experiment failed," he said. His expression turned serious. "Alison, the loft isn't big enough for you to set up your equipment, as you call it. The way I see things, you can either sleep or do your painting in the loft. So, since you're going to need your sleep if you want to be awake enough to paint, I'd like to offer you this room to use as your art studio."

"My art studio?" She blinked, not sure she had heard him right.

"Yes. That is, if you think it would be suitable. I can tell you that it'll be quiet here, and you can stash your supplies in the cabinet."

Alison looked around and began to see, not just empty space, but possibilities for transforming it into a studio, *her* studio. "I'd love to have the room, David." She turned, startled to find he'd drawn even closer to her. Gazing up, she asked, "Are you sure? I mean, are you certain Domingo and Rachel wouldn't mind? I'd be happy to pay for the use of it."

"I'm positive that Domingo and Rachel wouldn't mind. They'd be glad to know the place is being put to good use again. As for payment . . . " He held up his hand. "They wouldn't hear of it."

"Then I can't refuse your offer."

"Good!" Those warm brown eyes glowed with satisfaction. The next instant David turned away from her. "You wait here, Alison. I'll go up and get your artist's gear."

After he left, Alison walked over to the one window in the room. It looked out over the backyard; there was an unobstructed view of David's *casa*. The home was attractive in appearance, like the man who lived in it. And she suspected that, like David, the *casa* too could be a distraction if she wasn't careful. Yet she was curious about the home, how it was furnished. She wondered what David did for a living. He must not earn a fabulously high income, or else wouldn't he have fancier digs?

When she heard footsteps coming down the hallway, Alison pretended she was inspecting the cabinet.

"Where would you like this?"

Alison peered over her shoulder at David. He held the case of supplies in his hand. "Let's see." She looked around. "Over there would be fine." She gestured toward the Formica counter.

"I'm sure now you're eager to get your things unpacked, but if you can spare a couple more minutes, I'd like you to see the dining room and maybe the parlor."

Alison turned around. "Dining room?"

His face assumed that amused look again. "Didn't Rachel tell you dinner weekdays is included in your rent?"

"No, she didn't." Mingled with Alison's sense of puzzlement was relief. She hadn't relished the idea of eating fast food or grabbing a cold snack in the loft at the end of a busy day.

"Tomorrow night you can join us for dinner. Since this is Sunday, you'll be on your own for this evening."

Something he'd just said made her curious. "You mentioned *us*. Are there other boarders, that is, besides yourself?" How would she handle the prospect of just David and herself dining together each evening? And who would do the cooking? The images that conjured up caused her to smile.

"Matter of fact, Alison, there is," David told her. "A gentleman named Tom Paige. He's lived here since his wife died. He was eighty in July."

That was a month ago. Alison couldn't help but think of elderly Mr. Cormant who lived in the apartment across from hers in Cincinnati. He was a fine person, but very forgetful. The last time she'd visited him, he had dozed off in the middle of their conversation. "I see," she said. "I'll look forward to meeting him."

"Tom's anxious to meet you too. And, by the way, so is Lucy."

"Lucy?"

David motioned for her to come with him again. As they retraced their steps down the hallway, he told her, "Lucy's the cook and housekeeper." At the opposite end of the hall, he opened a door on the left and led Alison into the dining room. "Lucy's a terrific cook," he went on, "but I have to warn you, she's the mothering type."

Alison's heart caught on the word "mothering." She ducked her head to hide her emotions from David. "Why do you say that?"

"She reminds you to put your boots on after there's a snowstorm. And she asks if you've eaten your oatmeal on a blustery morning."

Glancing up, Alison saw that his eyes beamed with affection. "I'm certain I'll like Lucy," she replied.

"This will be your chair." David rested his hands on the back of one of the massive wooden chairs that were set around the dining table.

"Reserved seating, I see."

That drew a chuckle from him, and Alison laughed too. Then he moved away from the table. "I've taken up enough of your time for today."

Alison thought that he must want to get back to his weeding. "I should apologize. I took you away from your yard work."

"No. I was finished."

"Oh. Well, you must have other things to do." She shifted uncomfortably.

"Nothing that's pressing."

Alison smiled tentatively. "Thanks a lot for the tour, David."

"It was the most fun I've had in a long time." He had

to be kidding, of course, but he didn't act like it. "I'll show you the parlor another day."

"I'd like that."

David seemed reluctant to leave. When he finally moved to go, his fingers brushed hers. It must have been unintentional on his part, but the fact registered at once in Alison's mind that David's hands were definitely warm. "When I was young, my parents and I lived in a house that had a parlor," she volunteered, more, she was certain, to cover her discomfort than to hold David there.

But he stopped and turned back to her. "Did you?"

"Yes. It had a stone fireplace and bookshelves full of books. And there was a huge comfy chair where I would curl up with my blanket and my favorite doll. It was a cozy place to be on a winter night."

"Winter nights in Taos get very cold." The way David said it made the simple statement seem profound. Then, as if he'd just remembered that he was her landlord, he said in a strangely formal voice, "By the way, Domingo told me that you'd paid your rent in advance."

Fishing in his jeans pocket, David produced a ring with two keys on it. "You'll need these," he said with a smile. "The larger one is for the front door, the smaller one is to your loft." He handed the ring to her.

Her hand closed around the keys. "Thank you again, David, for everything."

His face broke into another smile. "I'll see that Lucy gets a stool for you to use in your studio. You can find your way back to the loft?"

"No problem."

There was an awkward pause as they continued to look at each other. Then David started off down the hallway.

This time, Alison purposely turned away so that she couldn't see him and headed for the utility room-cum-studio. She figured she'd have enough unpacking and organizing to do to keep herself busy for the afternoon and the better part of the evening.

As she set about removing her many tubes of paint from the suitcase, Alison considered that altogether it had been an interesting day. If she was less than impressed with what she had seen of New Mexico, she was nonetheless taken with the peaceful atmosphere of the Ramirezes' rambling old house. The abode had charm, an enchantment of its own, she decided. It was the kind of place she could soon feel at home in. That was, if she didn't see too much of the man who lived in the *casa* out back.

Chapter Two

The next morning Alison rose early to shower and dress. She'd enjoyed a good night's rest just as she had anticipated, though the stillness of the old house had bothered her at first and she'd lain awake longer than she should have, listening for the occasional gust of wind that set up a moaning sound around the corner of her loft.

After David had left her in the afternoon, she had neither seen nor heard any other signs of life before going up to her room for the evening. She had thought that she might run across the older tenant David had spoken of or catch a glimpse of Lucy going about her duties. But the place had appeared deserted. When she had finished storing away her supplies, it was nearly dark outside. And in the silence that had fallen about her like the night itself, she'd retreated upstairs feeling very alone.

In the warm stream of sunlight that spilled through the window, Alison found the loft a more cheerful place again. Despite any previous reservations, she was ready to begin exploring the town. Paul had recommended a walking tour as the best way to get to know an area, and she intended to take his advice. Taos must have something attractive about it. Why else had such a great number of artists decided to locate here?

After a shower and a shampoo, Alison twisted her hair into a braid. She slipped into the fresh pair of jeans and blouse she had selected the night before. Then she retrieved her knapsack from the closet and headed down the steps toward her studio.

Traversing the hallway, she noticed the house was still utterly quiet. Half expecting to see someone, she glanced over her shoulder. Just who was it that she hoped to run into?

A glimpse through the window of the old utility room told her. David's *casa* was framed in the square of glass and, with it, David himself. He was standing outside his front door. But he wasn't alone. He was accompanied by a dog, a handsome-looking cocker spaniel. Alison drew a couple of steps closer to the window, careful to keep herself out of David's sight.

She watched as David tossed something across the expanse of lawn. The spaniel bounded after the object, then raced back to its master. Alison decided the object was a Frisbee, which the dog dropped at its master's feet.

When he reached down to pat the spaniel's head, Alison noted that David had on a pair of jeans and a white shirt. Even from a distance his attractiveness demanded her attention.

The little drama ended abruptly with David striding back into his *casa*, the dog fast at his heels. Alison felt a stab of disappointment. She chalked it up to her wish for a better view of the spaniel.

She told herself she shouldn't be so interested in either the animal or its master. But as she gathered her sketchbook and pencils and put them into her knapsack, Alison replayed the brief, cozy scene in her mind. It made her smile.

"That's her, Esther. Isn't she gorgeous?"

Alison glanced toward the two elderly women who were seated the next table over at the outdoor café where she'd stopped for lunch. She had been idly eavesdropping on their animated conversation while she ate a tuna salad sandwich and sipped iced peppermint tea.

The woman who'd spoken was clothed in a smart lavender pantsuit. She pointed a red-tipped finger toward the sidewalk that bordered the tables. "Over there, Esther. That's Delphinia Rios."

"Oh, she's gorgeous, Amelia, absolutely stunning," the woman named Esther gushed, voice quavering slightly.

Alison couldn't help but follow the two women's gazes. A tall woman with long, flowing dark hair, and wearing a pink, low-cut sundress, was making her way through the crowded dining area. Slinking might be a better word Alison decided, though it was true that the woman was extraordinarily beautiful.

Delphinia Rios. The name sounded like it belonged to a movie star. As the woman passed by several of the tables, she smiled a greeting at the diners seated there. A distinct murmur arose in her wake. If Ms. Rios wasn't a movie star, she must at least be a very important person in Taos.

Alison glanced at Esther and Amelia. They appeared awestruck by Delphinia Rios. Amelia spoke first. "I understand she's seeing a younger man." The comment was made in a mock whisper that Alison easily overheard.

Esther's face lit up with obvious delight. "Well, Amelia dear, I can understand why. If I had been that well preserved at forty-four, I might have considered such a fling myself." Her husky voice sounded a definite note of envy.

Amelia tittered. "I don't doubt it. Either of us should have looked that good in our middle years." She sighed.

"From the rumors I hear, her young man is only in his twenties. And very handsome, of course."

"Of course," Esther echoed. "His name?"

Another sigh. "No one seems to know. But I will find out," Amelia promised resolutely.

"Maybe if we were to stay for a bit, order another cup of tea, he might put in an appearance."

"We don't have time. Did you forget that we're due at the club in fifteen minutes?" Amelia's tone was mildly scolding.

"It wouldn't be proper for us to be late, would it?"

"No, Esther, I'm afraid it wouldn't."

Alison smiled indulgently to herself. The older ladies no doubt thrived on their gossip. Yet she couldn't stop her own eyes from searching the crowd for another glimpse of Ms. Rios.

She was rewarded when she saw the woman being shown to a table for two not far away. It seemed her "young man" would be joining her for lunch. For a moment, Alison pondered whether she should wait and see what he looked like. Was he as handsome as David? She promptly chided herself for letting David into her mind again.

As Esther and Amelia rose from their table, she was tempted to ask them who Delphinia Rios was. But she didn't want them to think she was being nosy. Besides, she should be on her way too. The afternoon was half over. There was still a small cemetery that she wanted to explore, though she wondered if it would prove as interesting as the café.

The cemetery, named St. Ignacio's, wasn't far from downtown, but to Alison it seemed a world away. After jostling with hordes of tourists that morning, all eager to tour the Bent Museum and Kit Carson House, she was ready for any solitude the graveyard might offer.

Approaching, she saw that a mortar wall surrounded the plot. A marker by the wall informed her that St. Ignacio's Church, built in 1730, had originally stood beside the cemetery.

She ran her hand over the mortar. In places it was pockmarked with shallow holes. In others it was as smooth as glass. Along the bottom, wild daisies and small blue flowers grew in profusion.

Alison took her sketchbook from her knapsack and made a quick drawing of the scene. Then she let herself into the cemetery through the wall's wooden gate.

Already charmed by her first view of the yard, Alison began to walk among the tombstones. She stopped often to bend down and read an epitaph or to make a sketch. Most of the slabs bore inscriptions that revealed that the individuals buried there had died in the last century.

The center of the yard was dominated by a large crypt with the name Rodriguez etched across the top. Like so many of the other graves, it had fallen into disrepair. Though her sketchbook held a few good drawings from her morning's adventure, nothing had captured Alison's imagination as much as St. Ignacio's. She hoped she could do justice in a painting to the yard's serene beauty.

When she came to the last row of stones, she found they were in slightly better condition. Maybe it was because of the shelter provided by a copse of evergreen trees.

One tombstone in particular stood out from the rest. It was the largest in the row. As she knelt beside it, Alison noted there was an intricately carved rose in its center. She read the epitaph. "Rosa Novato Chapman. Born May 10, 1884. Died September 12, 1904." September 12 was only a few weeks away.

Making a quick calculation, Alison discovered that the woman named Rosa was just twenty when she died. What had taken her, Alison wondered. Certain illnesses were rampant then that were easily curable now. Perhaps the young woman had contracted pneumonia or diphtheria. There was another possibility. Rosa Chapman might have died in childbirth.

Alison caught sight of a second inscription near the base of the stone. "Angel of Mora," she read under her breath. *Angel of Mora.* What did that mean? Was it a cryptic religious message or a title of some sort? Suddenly Alison had a strange feeling that if Rosa Chapman were alive, she would have an interesting story to tell.

A ray of sunlight filtered through one of the trees, softly diffused. Dust particles floated through the stream of light, sifting silently down onto the grave.

Though she was more than intrigued by her discovery, a check of her watch told Alison she would have to head home if she wanted to freshen up before dinner.

Rising, she brushed off her jeans and stepped carefully around the gravestones. Just before she let herself out the gate, she took a last look behind and promised herself she would return soon.

Alison did have time, but barely, to shower and put on a fresh pair of jeans and a sleeveless cotton blouse. As she dashed on some lipstick, she told herself she was bothering only because the color complemented the blue shade of her top. It had nothing to do with the fact she would see David at dinner.

When she went down to the dining room, she was greeted by an older man she knew must be Tom Paige.

He introduced himself as such, giving her a dazzling smile as he got up to help her with her chair. Alison was impressed by his obvious vigor and thought that he hardly resembled Mr. Cormant at all, except for his shock of white hair.

Tom was tall like David, though not as lean. In any case, he didn't look eighty years old. "Here comes Lucy," he said, motioning toward the dining room door.

An Hispanic woman Alison guessed to be about sixty came bustling over to the table. Her arms were filled with platters and bowls. Steam rose from the dishes as she set them down. Alison saw scalloped potatoes in one bowl, sliced green and yellow squash in another.

"You must be Alison," the woman said, smiling.

"Yes. And you're Lucy."

"That's right. David said he'd told you about Tom and me." Lucy set a platter near Alison's plate. "I hope you like smothered steak."

"Very much." A tempting aroma wafted from the meat and gravy.

"Good." Lucy's eyes met Alison's again. "Well, enjoy your meal. I'll be back with some rolls. They're almost browned."

Alison watched Lucy hurry away, then turned to Tom. He was regarding her closely.

"David tells me you're an artist," the older man said as he lifted the platter of steak and held it out to Alison.

The mention of David's name made Alison acutely aware of the empty chair set up against the table. It must be David's. Was he late? Or not coming at all? She said to Tom as she took a piece of steak, "Yes, that's right. Or at least I try to be an artist."

In turn, Tom handed her the bowls of potatoes and squash. He clucked softly. "My wife, Elizabeth, rest her soul, used to dabble in painting. She did the two that hang in the loft." He looked for Alison's response as he cut off a bite of his steak.

"I saw them yesterday," she replied. "They're really colorful, vivid."

He gave her a smile. "Elizabeth would have been glad to hear you say that. In my opinion, they were some of her best. She used to work mostly in oil, but later she tried her hand at watercolor."

"That's interesting, Tom. I do most of my paintings in

watercolor and a technique called gouache." Alison watched his expression as she lifted a forkful of the potatoes to her mouth. The potatoes were delicious.

The older man raised a bushy eyebrow. "Gouache? It sounds like something improper."

Alison laughed. "I assure you it's very proper. I'll show you sometime." She turned the conversation to questions about his life with Elizabeth. As he put down his fork and leaned back, Alison had the feeling she was about to be entertained.

"Elizabeth was as much of an adventurer as me. You could say we enjoyed living close to the edge. But one time we got a little too close, even for Elizabeth." His eyes twinkled.

"How was that?" Alison laid aside her fork for a moment.

"We'd taken a trip up north to Colorado. Mind you, Colorado's a grand place to visit. But not in the month of January." He chuckled.

"You went in January," Alison guessed.

"I don't have any idea why." Tom scratched his head. "Young people take notions, I suppose. Elizabeth and I got bitten with the wanderlust. You could call us a pair of fools."

Fools in love, Alison thought, her heart contracting painfully.

At that moment, Lucy came in with the rolls. She put the heaped-up basket in the center of the table and left as quietly as she'd entered.

Tom went on, "We were heading up into those high mountains. The Rockies, that is. Our little Studebaker was brand-new and she was taking those snowy curves like a champion. That was, until we got to the top of Trout Creek Pass when ... " He stopped in mid sentence, his eyes drawn to the doorway of the dining room.

Alison turned to see what he was staring at. There was

David coming through the door. Her hands faltered for an instant; she clutched the corners of her napkin. But her eyes were on David, and it was apparent that his were on her.

Neither of them seemed able to look away. At last Tom cleared his throat, and it served to force Alison's attention back to the older man.

"As I was saying to Alison, it's about time you got home." Tom directed his remark at David. "You don't expect me to be entertaining this lovely young lady alone every evening, do you?"

Alison dared a peek at David. He was giving Tom a sheepish grin. She wondered if he might glance her way again. He didn't.

"Sorry, Tom," he said. "I won't have time to eat dinner with you this evening."

"Posh!" Tom waved his hand in the air. "What you need is a good meal to put some meat on those skinny ribs."

Alison might have announced that she thought David had just the right amount of meat on his ribs. She saved herself the embarrassment by turning her attention to her meal. She took a great deal of time cutting off a small portion of her steak.

"I'll grab a burger later. For now," David reached to the middle of the table and plucked a roll from the basket, "I'm sorry, but I've got a load of paperwork to catch up on tonight." Alison met his eyes—and saw that he was directing his comment at her. She nodded in agreement, even if she had no idea what paperwork he was referring to.

"If you aren't going to eat with us, at least take a couple more of these things to munch on," Tom insisted, shoving two of the rolls David's way.

David shifted the rolls to one hand and patted Tom's arm. "I'll be home in time for dinner tomorrow. Promise."

Alison couldn't miss the affection that passed between the two.

Heading for the door, David abruptly stopped. He turned back for a moment to say, "I doubt very much, Tom, that it would be a hardship for you to entertain this lovely young lady every evening."

With that he was gone, leaving Alison to stare after him. Her face felt flushed. It seemed from a distance Tom spoke to her, but she didn't catch his words.

"I'm sorry," she said finally. "What were you saying, Tom?"

Tom motioned for her to come close. She leaned as far over the table as was proper. With a furtive glance toward the doorway, he said, "I was just giving my opinion that what David should have is a good wife to take care of him."

"Why . . ." Alison tried to finish the sentence and failed. "What makes you say that?" Her voice sounded strained.

"Doesn't take care of himself, that's why. Always busy with his patients." Tom shook his head sadly.

Patients. That meant David was a doctor. She never would have guessed it. Before she could ask what kind of practice David had, the older man scowled in a disapproving way. "It's a shame, that's what it is. Since that young woman of his left him, there's been nothing for him but his patients."

Any questions about David's profession fled as Alison repeated, "Young woman?" She hoped her voice had returned to normal. "Was he . . . married before?"

Tom gave a snort. "No. Planned to be, though, I reckon." He toyed with his knife, examining the blade at some length. "You see, Alison, he and this girl—her name was Eileen—dated through high school. A case of puppy love, some said. When David graduated, he went off to California to college. Eileen promised to wait for him."

Alison clasped her hands together tightly under the table. "Eileen didn't keep her promise?"

"She might have. Her parents had other ideas." Tom let the knife drop. It landed on his plate with a loud clatter, startling Alison. But Tom smiled. "Eileen came from a well-to-do family. David didn't."

"I see." Alison thought she was beginning to understand. "Did you know Eileen?"

"David brought her over several times. He was a friend of the Ramirez boy, Martin."

"Yes. He told me."

"Did he?" Tom appeared pleased. "Anyway, Eileen was a pretty little thing. Like you. Only you're prettier," he added.

The comparison made Alison suddenly uncomfortable. She was sure she was blushing. "Thank you," she said to the compliment, not knowing how else to respond.

"You're welcome." Tom grinned at her. "Eileen seemed nice enough," he continued, "but her parents were determined to break up the romance. They sent her off to some fancy school back east. Wesley, or some such name."

"I believe it's Wellesley."

Tom shrugged. "Whatever. A couple of years ago, just before David came back home, Eileen's engagement was announced in the local paper. A fellow from New York. Seems his father's the president of some big bank."

"And you think David's still not over her?"

"Don't really know," Tom admitted. "He doesn't talk about it. Another gal chased him for a while, but he didn't take to her. David's like a son to me," he confessed, voice lowered. "I'm real fond of him. I'd like to see him find someone and settle down. It's what he needs."

Alison wanted to ask Tom how he knew what David's needs were. Maybe David was like herself. Maybe he had decided his career was all that mattered now. Maybe he was even happy with his decision.

"Well, I'll be! He's back."

Alison watched as Tom rose quickly from his chair and went over to the window. What was it he saw? Had David changed his mind and returned? Curious, she got up and joined Tom.

"Look. Right there." Tom pointed out the window.

Alison looked, but saw nothing. "I'm sorry. I don't seem to see . . . "

"There!" Tom sounded just the least bit impatient.

Alison squinted. Still nothing. If David were outside, surely she would notice. Unless he'd already passed the window and was on his way in.

"It's Nubbins."

"Nubbins?" Alison was beginning to wonder if Tom Paige might have too keen an imagination.

"He usually comes in the morning, but I told him there would be a young lady at the supper table tonight. He's come to make your acquaintance." Tom winked at her.

Alison smiled at the older man. He was a charming person, even if Nubbins was someone—or something—that existed only in his mind. To indulge him, she peered outside again. To her surprise, she saw movement in the branches of a tree that was close to the window. All at once, a fur-covered head poked its way through the leaves. Nubbins was a squirrel!

"Oh, he's adorable, Tom." She loved animals, all sorts, and from the looks of it so did her dinner companion. Very briefly, she wondered if David did too.

"I'll have to go out and feed him, you know. He's a bit spoiled."

An idea struck Alison. "Tom, would you excuse me for a minute? I'd like to get my sketchbook and do a drawing of you and Nubbins. That is, if you wouldn't mind."

"You'd want to draw an old codger like me?" He fairly glowed.

"You're far from an old codger," she retorted. "Yes,

I'd love to draw you. But only if you promise to tell me soon what happened when you and Elizabeth went up Trout Creek Pass.''

Tom shot another wink her way. ''It's a deal.''

Alison laughed, but as she hurried off to retrieve her sketchbook, all she could think of was David and the girl he'd loved who had married someone else. She wondered if Eileen was happy now, or if she regretted her decision. Alison already knew how she would feel. And it troubled her.

Chapter Three

Alison watched as the slightly built man eased himself out from under the Taurus.

"It's a busted transmission hose, just like I thought. Leaked most of the fluid, Ma'am."

"Oh, swell." Alison threw her arms up in a helpless gesture. "I leased this car just a couple of days ago. Who would think this would happen?" The unexpected breakdown showed promise of ruining what had started out as a perfect day for a trip into the Sangre de Cristo Mountains.

"I wish I could fix it for you, but the best I can offer is a ride back to Taos." The man shrugged apologetically.

It seemed she had no choice but to take him up on his offer. Of the few drivers who had passed her on the road, he was the only one who had stopped. Alison regarded him. He looked trustworthy, in his coveralls and yellow baseball cap, but how could she be sure? What she did know was that it was at least thirty or forty miles back to town. And the man's battered pickup truck appeared to be her ticket there.

She was debating what to do when a dark blue car approached. Rather, it was a Jeep. She couldn't see the driver, but she watched as the Jeep ground to a stop on the gravel shoulder just ahead of her disabled car.

A man got out. Alison blinked in recognition—and disbelief. "David!"

He looked at her, that smile of his spreading across his face as if he had expected to find her in just such a predicament. He was dressed casually again, in jeans and a red crew top. "I have to admit the surprise is mutual, Alison," he said at last. He regarded her car. "What happened here?"

Before Alison could respond, the man in the coveralls spoke up. "Busted transmission hose. She's lost most all her fluid," he explained again. "Seems you two know each other." He nodded at each of them in turn.

"You could say that," David replied.

"Well, regardless, she'll have to be towed," the man declared.

David got down on his hands and knees and peered under the car. "Looks that way," he called up.

"This gentleman offered me a ride back to Taos," Alison announced as David got to his feet. She wondered how David would respond to the news.

He turned to her, resting one hand on the hood of the Taurus. "Where had you planned on going?"

"No place in particular," she replied, still trying to absorb the fact that David Grier was standing next to her. "I'd thought I'd take a short trip into the mountains to do some sketching," she added.

"Ah, I should have known that." The way he said it rankled her just the least bit. He crossed his arms. "You can go back to Taos, if you want. Or you could spend the rest of the day with me."

Spend the day with him? It was a ridiculous notion. And the look on his face seemed to indicate that he believed she would take him up on it. But all she could think to say was, "You're going to stay up here?"

"Not right in this spot." David's sense of humor was apparently intact, whatever her mood at the moment might be. He glanced at his watch. "Actually, I was due in Valera about thirty minutes ago."

Alison knew what she should do. End it right there and say that she appreciated his offer, but she had decided to return home. Instead, she inquired, "Valera?"

"It's a village about twenty more miles down this road, then five miles down a dirt road."

The man who had stopped to help came forward.

Alison immediately turned to him. Now was the time to tell him she was going to ride back with him. "I'm sorry," she said. "Excuse me for a second. I have to get my purse."

She went around to the driver's side of the Taurus. David followed after her. "You're not going with him, are you?" he whispered to her.

Alison regarded him coolly. "Why shouldn't I?" she whispered back.

"He's a complete stranger." David put his hands on his hips. "Just because he's been helpful doesn't mean he's a nice guy."

Alison glanced the man's way. She was grateful to see he was looking in the other direction. "The gentleman appears all right to me," she retorted, tempted to tell David that the two of them were hardly fast friends.

"For all you know, he could be a prison escapee," David returned.

She wanted to laugh. "I doubt that. Now if you'll excuse me, my ride's waiting."

David planted himself in front of her. "I'd rather you come with me."

With him effectively blocking any movement on her part, Alison considered her options. She could, no doubt should, put him in his place, tell him that it was not his decision to make. But with his nearness came a feeling of vague confusion as well. She was angry, but a part of her enjoyed David's outburst of protective concern.

Then David broke into a broad grin. "Do you know that you're beautiful when you're mad?"

"That's an old line, David."

"In your case it's true, Alison." Suddenly he grew serious. "You might think I'm being obnoxious, but I meant what I said. I wish you'd come with me to Valera."

Something about the way he said it, the silent appeal that she read in his eyes, softened her. She sighed. "Okay, but the least I can do is give the guy a token of my gratitude."

David stepped away from her. Alison drew a five-dollar bill from her purse and went over to the man. "I've decided to go with David after all," she explained, handing the bill to the man. "I want you to have this for your assistance."

When the man saw what she was trying to do, he started to give the money back to her, protesting, "I didn't do anything."

"You were a great help," David asserted, taking the bill from Alison and pressing it into the man's palm.

"Okay, I thank you," the man returned, smiling as he headed for his truck.

With a sideways glance, Alison said, "I hardly think he had evil intentions, David." She let it go at that. The decision had been made and whatever opportunities the day presented, she would have to make the best of it.

After she retrieved her knapsack and portable easel from the Taurus, she found David tying a square of white cloth to the antenna.

"When we get to Valera, we'll call your rental agency and tell them to send a tow truck. That is, if Bell of Valera is working today."

"What's Bell of Valera?" It seemed David talked in riddles.

"That's what everyone in the village calls their antiquated phone system."

"I see." Alison had to smile.

They walked together the few yards to the Jeep and she went around to the passenger side. Opening the door, Alison saw that she had something of a problem. Staring at her almost nose-to-nose was the cocker spaniel she'd seen with David in the yard.

"Hi," she said, cautiously extending her hand to the dog. It appeared to grin at her, its pink tongue lolling out of its mouth.

"Huffy! In the back."

At David's order, the dog cast doleful eyes toward its master and barked once. Alison felt the brush of silky fur against her arm as the animal obediently hopped over the back of the seat.

"Sorry about that," David offered. "Huffy likes the view up front."

"I could always sit in the rear, you know." Alison's glance slid from David to the spaniel.

David looked dubious. "That might be interesting," he quipped. Then he started the motor and steered the Jeep off the shoulder. Huffy barked again, as if to say it was about time they were going.

Settling herself in the seat, Alison realized that she had no idea why David was on his way to a remote village in the Sangre de Cristo Mountains. "Are you taking some time off from work?" she asked.

David laughed. "Hardly."

"Tom told me that you're a doctor."

"He did, huh?" David kept staring ahead at the road. "That's true, but my patients are of the four-legged variety."

That took a couple of seconds to register. "Oh. You're

a veterinarian.'' Despite herself, Alison liked the idea. And she liked the rugged profile David cut as he maneuvered the Jeep around a sharp curve. At once she distracted herself with the view out the window, though she asked, ''Why are you up here today? Don't you have a practice in Taos?''

''Yes, but twice a month I hold clinic in Valera.''

Too preoccupied with her own concerns, she hadn't considered that she might have inconvenienced him. ''I'm sorry if I've made you late for your appointments.''

''No need to apologize.'' One look at him told her he felt no pressure. ''I don't make appointments in Valera, though the clinic is supposed to open at ten. What I do is see patients as they come. Mostly I treat minor ailments and do immunizations. On occasion I perform surgery. In the afternoons I generally have appointments at the farms and ranches in the area.''

''This is beautiful country,'' she said. It was true. In contrast to the barrenness around Santa Fe, the rugged terrain here was thickly forested.

''And there's better yet to come. You won't have any trouble filling the pages of your sketchbook.'' David paused, shifting gears on the Jeep. ''You'll like the people of Valera, too. There's someone in particular I want you to meet.''

Just the way he said it caused Alison to turn her head. When she did, her eyes met David's for an instant. Instead of the stubborn expression he'd worn a short while ago, his face bore a look of warmth and affection. Not for her, she believed, but for the people he had spoken of. ''Is that why you were bound to rescue me?'' she asked.

''I think I'll let you figure that out for yourself.''

David's casual reply irked Alison, but not for long. The scenery was too gorgeous to be spoiled by an inner debate over the meaning of David's remark. First, she caught a glimpse of a green ribbon of valley tucked between distant peaks. Then the Jeep passed a jagged escarpment of rock that ranged so high Alison imagined it might pierce the bright blue dome of heaven itself. In time, the steep cliffs gave way to a more pastoral scene of emerald fields and wildflower meadows, dotted with grazing cattle and sheep.

With such a feast for the eyes, Alison barely noticed when David turned off from the main road onto the dirt road that he'd told her led to Valera.

After bouncing along the road's rutted surface for several miles, they came to a huddle of low buildings.

"That's Valera," David said.

A metal sign, its post bent, proclaimed that the village was indeed Valera, with a population of 350. David brought the Jeep to a stop in front of a large building. Unlike the others, which were fashioned of adobe, this building was constructed of wood.

"That's the community center," David explained. "The villagers built it themselves just over a year ago. It's the pride of the community, the heartbeat, you might say."

Alison could believe that, as isolated as Valera was. She was about to remark what a nice job the people had done when she saw several bronzed, barefoot children running toward the Jeep. They were shouting and waving.

"Oh, no. Here they come," David whispered.

As the children drew near, Alison heard calls of "Dr. Dave!" and "Where's Huffy, Dr. Dave?"

"I didn't know you had a fan club," she teased.

As they emerged from the Jeep, they were at once surrounded by the "club." At first, the youngsters' eyes were on David. Alison noted how he took the time to greet each one, calling them by name. Juan. Lupe. Manuel. He tousled a boy's hair, gave the two girls present a hug. Then he reached in his pockets and brought out a number of wrapped candies. He handed a piece to each child.

"Rosella's cat threw up last night," the little girl named Lupe announced.

"He did? We'll have to take a look at him, won't we?" David looked solemn, though he winked at Alison over the children's heads.

Juan eyed Alison curiously. "Who's the *gringa,* Dr. Dave?"

"Gringa?" Alison asked.

"That's you, of course," he said, though he obviously knew she understood.

"You always make things clear, David." She meant it sarcastically, but with six pairs of huge brown eyes staring up adoringly at "Dr Dave," the remark came out more as a compliment.

"This nice lady is Miss Hughes. She's a friend of mine, Juan, and she paints very pretty pictures."

David was capable of a compliment, too, it appeared. And he'd called her a friend. Observing Juan, she saw his face was open and eager. "Would you paint me one, Miss Hughes?" he asked.

Alison laughed. "Maybe, Juan. Yes, maybe I can."

"Me, too!" the others chimed in chorus.

"We'll see." How could she say no to such lovable children? "Are all the villagers this charming?" she asked as an aside to David.

He nodded soberly. "I'm afraid so."

"We'll tell everyone you're here, Dr. Dave, and that your friend's here too," Manuel offered.

"What would I do without your help, Manuel?" David said with complete sincerity.

The boy started giggling; it soon caught on with the others. Then they were all off on a spirited race to the cluster of houses.

As Alison watched, a streak of tan went by. It was a minute before she recognized the streak was Huffy running to catch up with his human friends.

She and David unloaded their supplies from the Jeep and carried them to the front door of the community center.

Outside, a plump, attractive young woman and an elderly, frail-looking man waited. David introduced them to Alison as Rosella and Ruben.

Ruben gave Alison a big toothless smile. Rosella spoke a soft ''hello.''

''I hear that Baltazar threw up,'' David said to Rosella. ''That's her cat's name,'' he explained to Alison.

Rosella laughed. ''Let me guess. It was Lupe that told you.'' She turned and said something in Spanish to Ruben. He laughed, too, and gave his knee a hearty slap.

Alison surmised Rosella had told him the news. Though there'd been just the four of them talking, she saw a number of people were headed toward the center. Some carried wire cages. A few had dogs on leashes. One man was leading a goat.

The goat suddenly reared and began to bleat. That served to set the dogs barking in noisy chorus. From somewhere came a terrible howl. It seemed David had a diverse practice, and it was past time for him to see his patients. Alison wished she could stay and watch.

''I'll show you around the center later,'' David said, drawing her attention back to him. ''You'll be okay on your own until lunch?''

''Sure.'' Gazing up at him, Alison wondered for an instant if he might change his mind and ask her to stay. He didn't.

''We'll eat lunch in the center,'' David went on with a smile. ''The ladies of the village take turns fixing the meal and Rosella serves. It's been more or less a custom since I've been holding clinic here.''

''What a kind custom.'' Why was it so hard to tear her eyes from him? As before, David seemed to have the same predicament. Finally he turned away. But Alison kept looking after him as he went inside. He was followed by a long line of people. They all appeared to be talking at once in a mix of Spanish and English, and the procession put Alison in mind of a festive parade. She tried to imagine the chaos that might reign inside for a few minutes while David set up his clinic.

A gentle tap on Alison's shoulder brought her around. Rosella was beside her. "I could show you our village, if you want," the young woman offered. "Valera is small and not very modern, but it's our home." She smiled.

Alison liked Rosella; she could imagine her cheerfully bustling about, serving others their noon meal. "I'd enjoy that, Rosella. Thank you."

The tour proved more fascinating to Alison than she had anticipated. It wasn't long before a number of pages in her sketchbook bore preliminary drawings, just as David had promised. The last and most interesting stop she and Rosella made was the tiny Valera cemetery. Like St. Ignacio's in Taos, the graveyard was quite ancient. Rosella revealed that a more modern cemetery was located a couple of miles outside of town, but Valera cemetery was the one that held the remains of the village's settlers.

As they examined a few of the tombstones, Alison remembered the place where Rosa Chapman was buried. Knowing it was improbable, she said, "Something I saw in a cemetery in Taos made me curious. I don't suppose you've ever heard of Rosa Chapman or the Angel or Mora?"

To Alison's surprise, Rosella's face took on a sudden odd expression; she quickly averted her eyes to a study of the ground. The air around them grew still, as if waiting too for Rosella's answer. With the lull, Rosella became introspective and didn't respond for a very long time. At last she said in a low, sad voice, "*Sí*, I have heard of her."

The admission made Alison wonder all the more what story lurked about the mysterious woman who had died so young. She was puzzled, too, why the mention of Rosa Chapman's name had such an effect on Rosella. Their first names were similar. Likely it was coincidence, Alison told herself. Still . . . "Could you tell me anything about her, Rosella? I don't mean to pry, but I was curious from the moment I saw that inscription on her gravestone."

But Rosella kept staring at her feet, and Alison began to regret having brought up the subject. Rosella sighed. "I think David would be the best person to ask about Rosa Chapman and the Angel of Mora."

Why David? Alison formed the question—silently. With disappointment, she sensed Rosella had said as much as she was going to on the matter. She responded, "I'll ask him when I have the chance."

Rosella's eyes silently met Alison's.

After leaving the Valera cemetery, Rosella excused herself with a gracious smile, telling Alison that it was time for her to go and prepare the noon meal.

Alison thanked her for the tour and, on her own, wandered back through the village. Her feet seemed to carry her of their own volition to the community center. She got her easel and set it up near the building. Then she began to work on a sketch.

As Alison worked, villagers trickled by, friendly and openly interested in what she was doing. Each one happened to know her name, and she concluded the children must have spread the news about her arrival.

Completing her drawing, she decided she might have time for another and went in search of a subject. She found it in the peaks that formed a backdrop to the village.

Nearby was an abandoned house with a huge, shady cottonwood beside it. A dark green, leafy vine curved up and around two sides of the crumbling structure. The old homestead could prove a worthy subject too, Alison decided. She set up her portable easel by the tree and went to work.

Soon she noticed from the corner of her eye that a small boy was watching her. He stood in the shadow of a building that once might have served as a toolshed.

"What's your name?" Alison asked softly, assuming the youngster was shy.

There was silence. "Miguel," he said at last.

"That's a nice name. Mine's Alison Hughes."

"I know," came the hesitant response.

Alison saw the child escape further into the dark shadows. Her heart went out to him. She had been bashful when she was young.

For a while she just kept working on her sketch. Finally she observed that Miguel had moved away from the shed and toward her.

"You know, Miguel, I really like to draw. I'll bet you do too." Glancing discreetly his way, she saw he took another tentative step. Maybe she had struck a responsive cord.

"I enjoy painting people and animals, and things like flowers and mountains. What do you like to make pictures of, Miguel?"

"My puppy."

His sincere answer almost caused Alison to blow it and look his way. She caught herself. "Puppies are lots of fun to draw." For a moment, she feigned intense concentration, brushing feather strokes across the paper with her pencil.

The boy came closer. "You're pretty good," he remarked as though he were a seasoned critic.

"Thank you, Miguel." She turned the slightest bit in his direction, but kept her eyes on her work. "I'm going to paint over this later. For now I'm just doing a drawing so I won't forget the scene. Do you think this needs to be made darker?" She pointed to the base of the mountains.

He didn't answer immediately. Alison supposed he was giving the matter serious thought. "Maybe. I colored a picture of the mountains. I made them pink and blue 'cause that's how they look when the sun's coming up."

"They do? That sounds pretty. And I'll bet your picture

of them is very nice." Cautiously Alison turned until she was at last facing Miguel. She held out her hand to him.

He gripped it in his own small brown hand. She had won him over. "Juan told me that you make pretty pictures, Miss Hughes."

"Juan is your brother? I met him earlier."

"He's *one* of my brothers."

"How many do you have?"

"Five."

"And sisters?"

"Two."

"I think it would be neat to have that many brothers and sisters. I don't have any."

"You don't?" He sounded incredulous.

The more she looked at him, the more Alison was convinced that Miguel had to be the most beautiful child she'd seen yet in Valera. Maybe it was because of the kinship she already felt with him.

"If you want, sometime I could show you the drawing I did of Skeezer. He's my puppy."

"I'd like that very much."

Miguel acted hesitant to leave for some reason, so Alison resumed feathering in her sketch. It was only after she knew he'd left that she glanced back. What she saw caused a lump in her throat, and she understood why he had hidden from her. Miguel walked with a pronounced limp, his body leaning awkwardly to one side to compensate for the leg that was far shorter than the other.

Preoccupied with thoughts of Miguel, she finished her sketch and packed up her supplies. Her watch told her it was almost noon, time to meet David for lunch. She had lots to tell him.

Chapter Four

Lunch was a spicy dish called *Carne Adovada*, which David described to Alison as Mexican marinated pork. She tasted the dish and pronounced it delicious.

She and David were seated at a table alone. A number of the villagers, mostly older people, occupied tables in the large main room of the community center. A steady hum of conversation filled the air. The atmosphere struck Alison as cozy, like that at a family reunion.

As they ate, she asked David about Rosella's cat.

"The prognosis is good for Baltazar. He had a hair ball," David replied with a grin. "How was your morning? Did you find anything of interest to sketch?"

She told him that she had and described the tour Rosella had given her. "I found the cemetery especially intriguing," she said. "I like to snoop around old graveyards. Sometimes I make tracings of the stones." She thought of the ornate slab that marked Rosa Chapman's grave.

David's response was a curious look, as if he found the idea strange.

That put Alison off and though she had intended to ask him about the young woman called the Angel of Mora, she decided the timing wasn't right. Another day, she told herself. "I met the most adorable little boy. No doubt he's part of your fan club too. His name is Miguel."

David looked pleased. "So you got acquainted with my special friend."

"He's the one you wanted to introduce me to?"

David nodded. He was silent a moment as he concentrated on tearing a tortilla in half and buttering it.

Alison brought a spoonful of stew to her mouth. It felt very hot going down. "How old is he, David?" she asked.

"Ten."

She was surprised. "Miguel's very small for ten. He told me he likes to draw."

David chewed thoughtfully on a piece of the tortilla. "Miguel's a unique child, Alison. Sensitive, intelligent, empathic."

"Different in a way from the others."

"Yes, but not just because of his handicap." David peered at her earnestly across the table. "He has a perception of things, of people, that amazes me at times. And he's extremely gifted. He's shown me a number of his drawings. Even an untrained eye like mine recognizes that kind of talent."

"Is that the reason you were so anxious for me to meet him?" Alison wasn't certain she wanted to hear David's answer.

"Partly." David set his spoon down and wiped his mouth carefully on his napkin. "When I first started coming to Valera, Miguel asked me if he could be my assistant."

"I think I know your response, David."

He smiled. "First, let me tell you something about Miguel. He lost his parents. They were killed in an accident when he was three.''

''How . . . tragic.'' Alison cast her eyes down to a study of her plate.

''What is it?'' David asked softly.

''I lost my mother when I was very young. I was seven when she died of cancer.''

David touched her arm. ''I'm sorry, Alison. Your father?''

It appeared that David had a tender side. ''Dad's very much alive. He's wonderful. He taught me how to keep house, to cook.'' She thought of the distinguished-looking man who still called her his ''little Ali.''

David's eyes gazed into hers, full of sympathy. ''Then you weren't a *huérfano*.''

''*Huérfano?*''

''It's the Spanish word for orphan. That's what I named my dog because I found him abandoned by the side of a road not far from here. I call him Huffy for short.''

''And Miguel is a *huérfano* too.''

''Yes. His mother's sister took in Miguel and his siblings,'' David explained. ''Her name is Manuela. She's a good woman, kind. So is her husband, Raúl. But it's been tough for them economically. They're poor, don't have any children of their own. Suddenly having to provide food, clothing, and shelter for eight kids has made circumstances nearly impossible for them. But they manage.''

Alison tried to imagine the hardships the couple faced. Yet she also felt a certain envy for the companionship the large family would enjoy together. Scanning the room, she saw no sign of Miguel, nor of any of the other children. ''Are Manuela and Raúl here today?'' she asked David.

''No. Usually it's the older ones that come to the center during the day. They have time on their hands, so they play cards, gossip, eat lunch. Raúl works weekdays in Eagle

Bend, a village ten miles away. Manuela is busy with chores at home."

"Then even in the land of *Poco Tiempo* there's a lot of work to be done." Alison said it with a smile and was rewarded with a smile from David. "You were about to tell me that Miguel became your assistant."

"Yes, I was." David paused. "Miguel helped me that summer while school was out. He was just eight years old, but he took his duties seriously. I discovered he had a large amount of empathy for others, and he was great with the animals too. He only needed some encouragement and guidance." David looked at her thoughtfully. "Alison, that's what he needs now to develop his artistic abilities."

She shifted uncomfortably. What was he trying to say? Was he expecting that she would be the one to fill Miguel's "needs?" Already she was far too fond of the young boy, but she hadn't come to New Mexico to take up tutoring. "What about his teacher at school? Surely he, or she, would encourage Miguel in his drawing?"

David shook his head. "This whole area is poor. The children attend a rural school where they teach just the basics, no frills."

"No art instruction?" she asked, astounded.

"Afraid not."

"But that's . . . " She didn't get to finish.

Rosella appeared at the table with a shy smile and an apology for not having asked sooner if they wanted more stew. They didn't. She smiled again and told them she would bring their dessert.

David thanked Rosella, then turned his attention back to Alison. "As you were saying about the Valera school system."

Alison straightened under his gaze. Why did he seem to have the knack for making her feel alternately at ease and uncomfortable in his presence? "You're probably going to consider this a prejudiced statement, but I don't view art instruction as a frill. I think it's a shame they can't find room in the school budget for an art teacher, even if it's just a part-time position.''

David grinned at her. "Prejudiced? Maybe, but I share your sentiments.''

Rosella appeared again, as promised. Dessert, she told Alison, was a type of creamy pudding in caramel sauce. It was called flan. She waited until Alison took a bite and praised the dish. Then, with a nod of the head, Rosella excused herself.

Alison decided the break was a good opportunity to change the topic of conversation. "Do your parents live in the Taos area?''

"No. Dad owned a small printing business in Taos for years. He built up a good clientele. But after my sister, Beth, got married and moved to Los Angeles, Mom and Dad went for a visit. They liked California a lot. I was there at the time, too, living with Beth and her husband while I attended UCLA.''

"That's where you got your degree in veterinary medicine?''

David nodded. "Like I said, Mom and Dad came out. They enjoyed the climate and ocean so much, they decided to move to the West Coast. Only they went farther north, above San Francisco, to a small town called Ukiah. Dad reestablished his business there, though it's just a shoestring operation.''

"But you didn't stay in California.''

David fidgeted with his napkin for a moment. "No. Not that I didn't enjoy the climate myself.'' He looked reflective.

Alison recalled her conversation with Tom Paige. He'd said David had planned to marry the girl named Eileen, and that her engagement to another man was announced just before David returned to Taos. Should she broach the subject of his coming back? Would it stir painful memories of the past? She decided to chance it. "Why did you return to New Mexico and set up your practice in Taos and Valera?"

He took his time dipping his spoon in his bowl of flan. Then he looked up and smiled. "Remember the old saying, it's a long story?"

"Maybe you could give me the condensed version?"

That drew a chuckle from him and Alison felt a small sense of relief.

He fixed his gaze on the wall above her head. "It might be easier first to tell you how I knew I wanted to be a veterinarian. Of course, I was born and raised in Taos. A friend of the family, Edward Éstevez, was the town's lone veterinarian back then. And I was the kid who had a penchant for carting home wounded birds and stray cats."

"I was too," Alison confessed.

David's eyes met hers: they studied her face with a thoroughness that caused a sudden warmth in her cheeks. "I figured as much when you told me about meeting Miguel. The way you looked, the softness of your expression."

She averted her eyes until she regained her composure. "Children and animals have a knack for playing on our sympathies, don't they?" she said at last. "Now you were telling me how you became a veterinarian."

"That's right, I was. Well, whenever I brought home an injured critter, my mother would send me packing with it to Dr. Éstevez. He took my almost weekly intrusions with good humor. The summer I turned thirteen, Dr. Éstevez asked me if I'd like the job of feeding the clinic's patients and cleaning out their cages."

"You were his assistant."

David grinned. "I guess you could say that, and from that time on I knew I wanted to be an animal doctor. When I graduated from high school, I was given a scholarship to UCLA. As I said, Beth and her husband lived in L.A. They offered me room and board and I worked part-time—at a veterinary clinic, of course—to supplement my scholarship.''

''You came back to Taos then right after you graduated?'' For a moment Alison thought she saw a shadow of sadness in David's eyes, and she regretted asking the question.

''Yes.'' He ate the last of his flan and set the bowl aside. ''I had an offer to join a very lucrative small animal practice in the suburb of Riverside. I was tempted by it for a minute or two, but I knew Edward was ready to retire. I had always believed he would ask me to take over his practice. Which he did.''

''And you agreed because you didn't want to let him down?''

''To an extent, yes. But there were . . . other reasons. For one, the rural areas of New Mexico are in critical need of veterinarians. Besides, this is home, Alison.'' He raked his fingers through his hair.

The innocent gesture at once kindled in Alison feelings that she had no desire to acknowledge. To make matters worse, David's face took on a certain expression that made her think he knew what those feelings were. Not about to let him conclude that she found him unbearably attractive, she turned her head the other way and began to observe the villagers seated at the various tables.

Some of the tables were now empty, others still occupied by groups engaged in conversation or a game of cards. But one nearby assemblage of older ladies had their attention focused on something else of interest. With embarrassment, Alison saw they were watching David and herself.

The women's creased faces wore smiles, as if they were bestowing their silent approval on the veterinarian and his companion.

''Were you about to say something, Alison?'' he asked right on cue.

She raised her eyes to meet his. "I would imagine that you've grown fond of the people of Valera."

"Extremely fond," he replied, his eyes still on her.

There was the sound of a discreet cough nearby. Alison peered up to find Rosella standing at the table.

"I'm sorry to interrupt." She addressed David. "You have a phone call. José Flores."

"Thank you, Rosella." Turning to Alison, he explained, "One of my afternoon appointments. Excuse me for a moment."

Rosella sighed. "It's often like that with David. He comes to eat and before he's finished with his meal, one of the ranchers is calling, wanting to talk to him."

"He's very dedicated to his profession, isn't he?"

"He is," Rosella agreed. "David's been kind to all of us here in Valera. He's done many good things for us. He even . . . " Rosella stopped short; her hand came up to her mouth. "Please . . . excuse me, Alison. I forgot something in the kitchen. I must go."

Alison looked after Rosella, puzzled by the woman's abrupt departure, wishing she knew what Rosella was about to say. Then David returned and informed her it was time for them to leave on his rounds.

As they were packing up the Jeep, he said, "I'm sorry I didn't get to show you the rest of the community center. Another day," he added with a smile.

Alison avoided his eyes. "Yes . . . maybe."

"Yes, definitely." Before she could respond to that, he went on, "The phone call from José was about his mare. She's close to foaling and he's worried about her. He wants me to have a look at her today."

"We'll be going there?"

"I'm afraid so." David reached out and put his hand on her arm. "Alison, he lives a good distance from Valera, and I have two other appointments to keep today. That means we'll be getting back to Taos a lot later than I'd expected. I'm sorry, but I can't let the man be worried about his animal.'' His hand stayed where it was, fingers resting lightly on her arm.

She heard what he said, acknowledged it with a murmured, ''No, of course not. It's all right.'' But her attention was focused on David's hand, on the warm, gentle touch of his fingers on her flesh. He must have suddenly become aware of what he was doing for he drew his hand back.

''We'd better go,'' he said quietly.

When Alison went around to the passenger side, she saw Miguel standing by the door. Huffy was sitting next to the boy, tail thumping. ''Miguel!'' she said, pleased he was there. ''I hoped I would have a chance to see you before I left.''

He ducked his head and shoved a hand deep into his jeans pocket. ''I guess you and Dr. Dave have to go on rounds now.''

Alison couldn't help smiling. ''Yes, we do.''

Miguel looked up at her with huge eyes. Without warning, he thrust a piece of paper toward her. ''You said you wanted to see my drawing of Skeezer. He's not with me and Huffy 'cause he's home sleeping.''

Alison took the paper. It was wrinkled and there were smudges on it, but that wasn't what she noticed. The portrait that filled most of the page captured her eyes. She was amazed by the fine quality of it, the maturity that shone through in the artwork, considering that Miguel was a child and had no formal training. ''This is really good, Miguel. Wonderful, in fact,'' she said sincerely.

David came up to them. ''What's wonderful?''

''This.'' She handed him the portrait.

''Didn't I tell you?'' He looked at her over Miguel's head.

Ignoring the comment, she asked Miguel, ''Have you drawn a lot of pictures?''

"Probably about a hundred." He gazed up at David after he said it. David put his arm around the boy's shoulder.

Alison took in the look of adoration on Miguel's face. He turned to her. "If you come back with Dr. Dave, I could show you more pictures."

"I'm sure Miss Hughes would love to come back, but she's only going to be in New Mexico a few months and she'll be very busy with her own painting."

Bless you, David, thought Alison. The gratitude was short-lived. Between David's expectant expression (never mind what he'd said) and Miguel's wistful one, she felt like the victim of a conspiracy. "Maybe one day before I go home I could visit Valera again."

"Miss Hughes is an art teacher back home in Cincinnati."

David's small revelation caused Miguel's eyes to grow even wider. "A teacher? Wow! Would you teach me how to paint, Miss Hughes?"

"I'd like to, Miguel, but . . . I'm not sure if I would be . . . "

"I conduct clinic in Valera twice a month," David interrupted softly.

She felt the net draw tighter. "I believe you already told me that." She paused. "Perhaps I could . . . "

"You'll be my teacher then?" Miguel put in eagerly.

"I . . . yes, it looks that way, Miguel." She thought of something that could be her saving grace. "But won't school be starting soon, David? That would mean Miguel would be in class in the daytime."

David held up his hands. "That shouldn't be too much of a problem. I'll speak to the principal at Miguel's school." He beamed at her as he placed both hands on Miguel's shoulders. "I'm sure Mr. Suarez would be pleased to give Miguel half a day off every other week for private lessons."

Trapped. With that simple statement, it seemed that Da-

vid had worn down the last of her defenses. Yet, if she
were honest, Alison couldn't say that she was angry at him.
Irritated, as usual, perhaps. But she was too taken with
Miguel to feel any real sorrow over the commitment she
had made. And though she would not have admitted it,
even to herself, she was taken with David too. "It guess
it's settled, Miguel. We'll plan to have our first lesson in
two weeks."

"Oh, boy!" It was obvious Miguel could hardly contain
his excitement. His thin body shook for a moment. Alison
was tempted to sweep him up in her arms and give him a
hug.

David chuckled, then announced that they had to be on
their way. At David's command, Huffy jumped into the
back of the vehicle. Alison climbed into the passenger seat.

Miguel stood and watched them as they pulled out. David tooted the horn, and Alison waved. Miguel waved back.
Alison saw that he kept it up until the Jeep rounded a bend
in the road and they disappeared from sight.

Where the dirt road intersected the paved one, David
pulled onto the shoulder. The Jeep's motor idling, he turned
to Alison. His face came close to hers. "I realize you
thought I set you up back there. Maybe I did, though it
wasn't intentional. But I promise you won't be sorry that
you've given a young boy a chance he wouldn't otherwise
have had."

"No, I won't be sorry," she said, unable to keep herself
from smiling at David.

As they regarded each other, she became aware of his
breath against her face. It was warm and sweet. His gaze
moved to her mouth and lingered there.

Reason fled Alison's mind. She should tear her eyes from
his, turn away, make a joke. Anything to break the spell
that was weaving its way around them. But just when she
was certain that David would kiss her, certain that it was
exactly what she wanted, he pulled back.

He averted his eyes; his hands gripped the steering wheel. The Jeep was set in motion again. There was a dearth of conversation as the vehicle began to gain speed.

At last David spoke. "Our first stop," he said with some hesitancy, "is to see a pygmy goat that has a boil on its rump."

The remark came as such a surprise to Alison that she laughed. David laughed too. The tension between them was broken, and though a part of her felt cheated, Alison had to admire David's knack for defusing a situation that at least one of them was bound to regret later.

Chapter Five

The pygmy goat was attended to, and after that a horse with an injured hoof. Alison stayed in the Jeep with Huffy while David saw his patients. But she found herself an object of curiosity, just the same.

At the small ranch where the pygmy goat resided, several tiny children and a woman, whom Alison assumed was their mother, gathered around the Jeep. In halting English, the woman asked Alison her name, where she was from, and why she was with Dr. Dave. For some reason, her answers set off a fit of giggles in the children, especially the one about her car breaking down and David coming to her rescue.

At their next stop a young and very pregnant woman asked her the same questions all over again. She said her name was Marie, that her baby was due in two weeks, and that it was Dr. Dave who had found a midwife for her.

It was apparent to Alison that in Valera and environs David was considered something of a paragon. No doubt deservedly so, she told herself even as she watched him come toward the Jeep. He was carrying a large parcel, but that wasn't what Alison noticed. It was David himself, the confident air he projected as he strode across the yard from the ranch's stable. It struck Alison that he was someone who was perfectly at home in the majestic mountains of northern New Mexico. The isolated ranches, the village of Valera, were his environment and he thrived in it.

As he slid behind the wheel, David handed her the package. It was lumpy and tied with string.

"What's this?"

"That's payment," he replied mysteriously, though the corners of his eyes crinkled with humor.

"Payment?"

"Open it and you'll see."

She undid the string; the wrapping fell away, revealing several ears of corn, a large zucchini squash and two plump tomatoes. "Oh, instead of money . . . " She looked at David and smiled.

He regarded her, hands resting on the steering wheel. "Alison, to the people on these ranches, the animals are their means of livelihood. When a horse or goat gets sick or is injured, it can mean great economic hardship. Yet there may be no money in the budget for medical treatment." He traced around the wheel with one finger. "I set up an arrangement, you could call it, with some of my clients. I let them recompense me in other ways for services rendered."

"Produce from their gardens," Alison said, admiring the vegetables nestled in her lap.

"And sometimes a chicken or a dozen eggs."

"I'll bet Lucy's prepared more than one meal from your wages, David."

"You bet right," he said with a grin.

They headed out. Not far from the ranch David turned onto a rutted dirt road that, from all appearances, was no more than a path. The Jeep began to climb steeply, then veered around a sharp bend. Alison's view out the window was nothing but air and sky and a chasm that dropped straight down for what seemed miles. She gasped.

David chuckled. "Not to worry."

Easy for him to say. She attempted a shaky smile. "I'm . . . not quite used to such dramatic scenery." Laurel Gorge back home was child's play compared to this.

"We'll be past the dramatic part soon," he assured her.

And they were. After a few more twists and turns and gorges, they emerged onto a flat plain. There was a wide meadow, lush with crimson and yellow wildflowers. "How beautiful," Alison murmured.

"Yes," David agreed quietly. He brought the Jeep to a stop. "Over there," he said, pointing to a stand of trees nearby. "Do you know what they are?"

Alison had no wish to appear ignorant. "Skinny cottonwoods?"

David laughed. "A fitting description, but no, they're aspen. If we're lucky, in a couple of weeks they'll be starting to turn." He regarded her. "The leaves look like gold coins and sound like them too when a gust of wind comes along. It makes for a fairly dazzling show, unless there happens to be a hard freeze. Too much frost and the color's ruined."

Watching David now, the wind ruffling his hair, the sun on his face highlighting every chiseled feature, Alison could think of a view slightly more dazzling than the one he'd mentioned. But she would never tell him, nor allow herself to dwell on it a second longer. She turned away and looked at the trees again. "Would there be time on the way back for me to do a quick sketch of this meadow?"

"Plenty of time," came his answer. "First you have to tell me if you'd like to visit an expectant mare."

Though she replied only with a smile, Alison discovered that she did want to see the mare.

It turned out the animal was housed in a small but tidy barn on what otherwise appeared to be a ramshackle ranch. A short, heavyset man was waiting for them when they pulled into the yard. David introduced the man to Alison as José Flores. José gave her a smile, but his face bore a harried look.

He led the way to the mare with David following. Alison tagged along behind the two men. She wondered if José minded her presence.

The inside of the barn seemed dark to Alison, but after a minute her eyes adjusted to the dimness and she saw the horse. Its taut, swollen belly reminded her of Marie. She hoped that neither mother would experience a difficult delivery.

David asked if she'd like to watch the exam.

She declined and returned to the Jeep where she waited with a fast-asleep Huffy. When David came, Huffy stirred and gave a questioning bark before dozing off again.

"Is the mare all right?" Alison was surprised by the anxious tone of her voice.

David gave her a reassuring smile. "She's fine. The problem is more with José."

"Father-to-be jitters?"

David laughed. "An apt diagnosis, Alison."

On their way back, David stopped at the meadow. Alison made a quick sketch as he watched. His attention should have caused her to be self-conscious, but curiously she felt at ease, as if she were used to drawing in his presence.

"Very nice," he commented when she finished. "Are you planning on doing a watercolor of it?"

"Likely. First, I'll do a few more sketches, then study all of them before I choose a couple or three that look promising. It's a weeding-out process."

"I'd say that you're very selective." David consulted his watch. "We're not going to get back to Taos in time for dinner, I'm afraid."

"That's okay." It was strange; she hadn't even thought about being hungry. "Last night you said something to Tom about grabbing a burger. I haven't had a good hamburger in a while. Unless you'd rather not."

"I never get tired of hamburgers," David avowed. "And I know a place that puts other burger joints to shame."

It didn't seem long at all to Alison until they were well on their way out of the mountains. The gorges this time gave her no more than a tingle of apprehension. She was getting used to them. They came to the spot where she'd left her Taurus. It was gone.

"Looks like the rental agency came for your car," David remarked.

"Yes," she agreed. She might have added that her day had turned out much better for the breakdown.

After a few more miles, David swung the Jeep onto another paved road and then immediately into the parking lot of a cinder-block building.

Alison was certain the place must be visible from the other road, though she hadn't noticed it that morning. Now she saw a large sign with the words, SHELDON'S CAFÉ— HOME OF THE WORLD-FAMOUS MESQUITE BURGER.

"Mesquite Burger?" she asked David as they got out of the Jeep and headed for the door of the café.

"Uh-huh. When you taste it, you'll know that sign isn't lying."

With all the activity, Huffy had wakened and was following them to the door. Alison wondered if the dog was planning on having a burger too.

David whistled and Huffy stopped. "Around back, Huffy."

Obediently, the spaniel disappeared past the corner of the restaurant.

"Sheldon keeps Kibbles and dog biscuits in the kitchen for him," David explained.

"Sounds delicious. For Huffy, I mean."

David laughed heartily, then said, "Go in," as he opened the door for her.

Alison noted that the dining room looked neat and clean, if plainly furnished. Nothing fancy, just good food, she surmised from the inviting odors that greeted her nose.

A chubby teenager in tight black pants and a white blouse stood at the counter. She sauntered up to Alison and David, carrying menus in her hand. "What's up, Dr. Dave?" She flashed him a saucy smile and Alison a questioning look.

"Nothing much," he replied. "You keeping out of trouble, Gracie?"

"Sure." The girl led the way to a booth in the far corner of the café, though the place was empty of diners.

Gracie plopped a menu down in front of David, another in front of Alison. She leaned forward, jaw working madly. Before long, a huge pink bubble emerged from the girl's puckered lips and burst with a loud pop.

She seemed to study Alison for a moment. Smiling slyly, she said, "I've been good, Dr. Dave, but I'm not so sure about you. Who you got with you tonight? Another of your hot dates?"

Alison considered that Gracie could use a bit of a dressing down, but David seemed to be taking the teenager's insolent remarks in good humor.

"Gracie, this is Alison Hughes. She's an artist from Cincinnati who's boarding with us in town."

"Cincinnati, huh?" Gracie stared at Alison as though she were from outer space instead. "Isn't that in Arkansas or someplace?"

A grin broke across the girl's face. Alison realized the teasing meant she'd been accepted by Gracie.

"Okay, you guys." Gracie became all business. "What'll it be? Or would you like a couple of minutes?"

"A couple of minutes."

"Cool, Dr. Dave, but we just ran out of them."

David shook his head and rolled his eyes. Alison laughed at the corny joke. She decided she liked Gracie, after all.

"You'll get used to her if you come in here enough," David said after the girl had left.

Alison made up her mind to do some teasing herself. She peered around the room, as if scrutinizing it. "So, David, this is where you bring your hot dates."

"Only one, Alison," he replied swiftly, his eyes commanding her attention.

The totally unexpected response, the heat of his gaze, effectively derailed any comeback she might have had. Choosing to ignore him, Alison took her menu and studied it. Most of the menu's two pages was devoted to a listing of hamburgers and their varied condiments. Many of them had exotic-sounding names like the Maui Volcano Burger and the Shanghai Supreme.

Several of the concoctions sounded revolting, but one in particular caught Alison's attention: the Elvis Burger. The description read: *A 100% pure beef patty, cooked rare on the grill, topped with our own special peanut sauce and a sliced banana.*

"Ever had an Elvis Burger, David?" she asked casually.

He grimaced. "Once. I don't think I'll ever look at peanuts and bananas in the same way again."

Alison laughed. "I'll settle for the Mesquite Burger, then."

Gracie came back and took their orders, returning with two tall glasses of iced tea. As she set one of the glasses in front of Alison, she winked at her.

"Tell me why you chose to come to Taos to paint," David said after Gracie left them alone again.

"As you once said, it's a long story." That elicited a smile from David. "Basically, I teach watercolor at Glockner Art Institute and have since I graduated from there three years ago." Alison selected a packet of sugar from a bowl on the table, tore it open and poured it into her tea.

"Have you taken a leave?"

She stirred her tea. "No. A certain wealthy patron, Eliza Deaver, left her fortune to the school in the form of grants."

"And you received one of the grants," he guessed.

"That's right. I love my position at the Institute," Alison asserted. "They've been good to me. One of my instructors, who's now my friend too, helped me win the grant."

"Do you paint just in watercolor?"

"No. I also work in gouache."

David's reaction was much like Tom's. "Gouache?"

"It's a form of watercolor, actually. A technique using paints that have white added to them to make them more opaque." She warmed to the subject. "Some of the cheaper paints contain chalk, so to achieve a higher quality likeness, it's best to use paints with a medium called Chinese white mixed in."

"Defined like a true teacher."

David's expression of genuine interest told Alison that he hadn't been bored by her explanations. She was impressed. She found it rare for anyone outside her circle of colleagues to show such fascination for the subject. But was it her profession that intrigued him?

Before she had time to consider the question, Gracie came with their sandwiches. Alison was amazed that her burger covered half the plate. A mound of thick fries occupied the other half.

"Okay, you two lovebirds, will there be anything else?"

Alison chose to ignore the comment. David didn't.

"The lovebirds have been nicely taken care of, thank you," he quipped.

Alison wondered if this was another typical exchange between David and the teenager—assuming that he did bring his "hot dates" to the café, which she could hardly picture. Regardless, their day together, no matter how enjoyable, was in no respect a date.

She and David were busy for a few minutes with their burgers. The sandwich was too unwieldy to pick up whole, so she cut it in half. Taking a bite, she discovered the burger lived up to its fame. "This is delicious, David."

"What did I tell you?" He peered at her over his sandwich. "I have to warn you, though. Mesquite Burgers can be habit-forming."

It was a habit she wouldn't mind, Alison decided as she took another bite and rivulets of spicy sauce ran down her fingers.

David ate for a moment, then put his sandwich down. "I would guess there's someone special in Cincinnati who's missing you."

Alison almost dropped her burger. How did the man have such a knack for catching her off guard? *He's enjoying it,* she thought. *He likes to make me uncomfortable.* But David didn't look as if he were trying to make her uncomfortable.

"I'm sorry, Alison. I shouldn't have asked that."

Her annoyance at him fled. And she discovered that she wanted to tell him, though confiding in a man she scarcely knew was not her usual style. "It's all right," she said at last. "There was someone. His name is Erik VanMer and he's a sculptor from Cleveland."

"You're not together anymore?"

"No." Alison folded her napkin, unfolded it again. "We were planning to be married and then open a gallery together in Cincinnati. But Erik suddenly had other ideas. He decided we should go to Paris instead."

David watched her closely. "Paris didn't interest you?"

"I'd love to see Paris." *With the right person,* she almost said. "I just didn't feel that, at this point in my life, I wanted to uproot and go abroad." Did David think she was foolish for passing up such an opportunity? His expression was more sympathetic than critical. She went on, "I came to realize that Erik didn't place equal importance on our careers." She could have said a lot more on the subject.

"I understand."

Alison chose to believe that David was being truthful, further that he cared, that his question hadn't been asked out of idle curiosity. She could have started querying him about his own love life. *Leave it for another time,* she told herself.

"My painting is very important to me," she said. "Now I'm being given a chance to prove myself. Paul—he's the friend I mentioned earlier—has asked me to be in his show next spring. That could lead to a show of my own sooner than I'd ever dared hope for."

"That's fantastic."

There was no misinterpreting David's admiration. Not surprisingly, Alison found that she admired him too.

"We'd better finish our sandwiches," he reminded her, though he made no move to resume eating his.

Despite her earlier enthusiasm for the taste of the food, Alison found her appetite was gone. But she made an attempt and managed to down a few more bites.

Gracie appeared at their table just as they were pushing their plates aside. "You two want doggy bags for this stuff?"

Alison peered at the remains of her burger. The sauce had begun to congeal. "I don't think so, Gracie. Thanks just the same."

David shook his head. "I'll pass too." He excused himself for a moment, saying he wanted to check on Huffy and say hello to Sheldon.

"Sheldon's my Dad," Gracie explained when David left. "He owns this place and does all the cooking."

"Tell him I thought the Mesquite Burger lived up to its publicity on the sign out front." Alison smiled at Gracie, then took a sip of her iced tea.

Gracie grinned back. She dawdled at the table, watching Alison. Then she leaned over, beckoning for Alison to come near. "Take my advice, Alison, and grab him quick."

Alison almost choked on the tea. "Excuse me?"

Gracie looked impatient; her jaw worked furiously on the gum in her mouth. "Dr. Dave. He's radical, you know. Totally radical."

Alison perceived the remark as a high compliment. She suspected Gracie was the one who would like to "grab him quick," if she were just older. Alison regarded the teenager uneasily. "I appreciate the advice but . . . "

"Gracie!"

The booming voice echoed through the café. Alison drew in a sharp breath. Gracie jumped. "Gotta go, Alison. Remember what I said," she admonished before dashing away.

Alison sagged against the booth, but there was little time to recover before David was back.

"Are you all right?" He eyed her with concern.

She squared her shoulders and gazed at him evenly. "Fine. Why do you ask?"

"I don't know, just something about the way you looked." The next thing Alison knew, David's hand brushed hers. "It'll be dark soon. We need to head home."

He took her hand to help her out of the booth. They stood very near each other. "Tom won't be pleased that we've missed dinner, will he?" she said.

"Oh, I don't know that he'll mind too much. Particularly when he hears that we've just had ours together."

Alison had no reply for David, only a game smile as he retrieved the check, then led the way to the counter.

Chapter Six

The day after her trip to Valera, Alison was in possession of another Taurus, a white one this time. It was delivered that morning by the same courteous agent who had given her directions to Cortez Court. The man was full of apologies for any inconvenience that the breakdown of the other car had caused her.

Alison was just as quick to assure him that it had turned out to be not much of an inconvenience, though she didn't tell him the reason why. With a scratch of his head and a puzzled smile, the agent told her he was glad and that the replacement car had just been serviced and he hoped it wouldn't give her any trouble. Then he handed her the keys and bid her good-bye.

Despite her confidence that the new Taurus was reliable, Alison decided not to attempt another solo outing for a while. Instead, she focused her energies on beginning paintings from several of her sketches. One of the sketches she'd chosen was of Tom and Nubbins. Another was the scene of the mountains behind Valera that Miguel had lent her his advice on.

Determined to make the most of her time, she set up a schedule for herself. She would spend every weekday afternoon and evening in her utility room studio, painting. Mornings and weekends she would devote to finding new subjects to fill her sketchbook or in attending to necessary errands. One of those errands, she told herself, would be to purchase some basic supplies for Miguel. If the boy was to properly learn the techniques of watercolor, he must have the right tools.

Alison considered the obligation she had made to Miguel. Two days a month out of her proposed schedule wasn't much, she reasoned again. She knew David had been right. How could she regret devoting a few hours during her stay to helping a talented young boy? Already she suspected that she was going to benefit from the lessons in a way that would prove far more valuable than whatever she might teach Miguel.

No, it wasn't the idea of serving as a tutor that troubled Alison. But she knew a certain sense of restlessness, and the reason for it was elusive—or perhaps it wasn't elusive at all.

Since her unexpected jaunt to Valera, thoughts of David kept intruding on her mind. An image of him smiling at her over their lunch of *Carne Adovada* was the first thing that had come into her head on awakening in the morning. And, on several occasions during the day, she recalled the easy sound of his laughter, the way his eyes had commanded her full attention when he spoke of Miguel or explained why he had chosen to become a veterinarian and return to his hometown to set up his practice.

But her most vivid memory was of the moment in the Jeep when his face had come so close to hers, and she'd been certain he would kiss her. There was no question in her mind that she was attracted to David, more so than to any man in recent history—Erik VanMer included, if she were totally honest with herself.

It was that very magnetism David projected that set off an alarm in her head. There seemed no way of escaping him during her stay in Taos. So she would simply have to deal with his presence in as rational a manner as possible and remind herself that in a few short months she would be on her way home. And home—Cincinnati and the Institute, to be exact—was where she belonged.

That stratagem worked, at least to the extent that she was able to get a very good start on her painting. And it helped that, as the week passed, David didn't put in an appearance at any of the evening meals.

As she cleaned her palette and brushes late Friday afternoon, Alison contemplated the progress she had made. The watercolor of Tom and Nubbins was over half finished, and she was pleased with the way it was turning out. Her gouache rendering of the mountain scene was only slightly less completed. Though the backdrop of sky needed softening a bit, the piece was shaping up well. It might even be one she would choose to feature in Paul's show.

Glancing at her watch, Alison saw that it was nearly dinnertime. She hurried to finish cleaning her supplies. Then she stashed them away and went upstairs to change out of her paint-spattered smock into a knit top and matching shorts.

When she came down to the dining room, she saw that Tom was alone at the table. Her eyes were automatically drawn to David's empty chair.

"Looks like we'll have to put up with each other's company again," Tom remarked as he rose to help her with her chair. His assisting her had fast become a courtly ritual.

"Thank you, Tom," she said with a smile. "I don't know about you, but I'm finding the company very agreeable," she added. That elicited a mild chuckle from the older man.

Over their meal of fried chicken, salad, and corn on the cob, Tom asked about her painting. Alison noted the animated expression that took over his face as she told him that his portrait was coming along nicely and that she should have it ready for his inspection soon.

Lucy appeared to clear their plates when they were finished. She had just gone off to the kitchen to fetch their dessert when David came into the dining room.

"Well, at least you showed up for pie," Tom jested as David sank into his chair.

Alison thought David looked exhausted and more than a bit disheveled. His blue shirt, which no doubt had been perfectly pressed when he put it on, bore numerous wrinkles and a couple of stains. His hair was mussed, as if it had been hit by a strong gust of wind. She surmised he had come directly from work. Still, she found his appearance no less agreeable.

He gave Tom a tired smile. Then his eyes met Alison's and there was a subtle, but definite, change in his manner. Had Tom noticed it?

"Have you had a busy day at the clinic?" she asked, though the question seemed redundant.

David's smile broadened to a grin. "A busy *week*," he answered. He ran his hand slowly through his hair. The familiar gesture served to tame some of the wayward strands. "How about you, Alison? Has Tom been plying you with tall tales in my absence?"

"Fascinating ones," she returned, wavering just a fraction under his gaze. Actually, her conversations with the older man had been varied and stimulating. They had talked of her art, of how he and Elizabeth had met, the places they'd lived and visited, the fact the couple had never had children, yet had enjoyed a happy and prosperous life together.

There was one story he hadn't finished telling her. Alison turned to the older man. "That reminds me, Tom. You never said what happened the time you and Elizabeth went up Trout Creek Pass in your new Studebaker.''

Tom looked pleased that she'd remembered. ''I'll be. I didn't, did I? Here I've kept you hanging all this time.'' He laughed.

Lucy reappeared at that moment with the pie. She set a bowl in front of each of them. Alison saw that her dish held a large wedge of apple pie topped with an immense scoop of vanilla ice cream. The combination looked sinfully delicious.

''Mmm. My favorite,'' David said to Lucy. The woman smiled, ducking her head shyly at the compliment.

''Tell you what,'' Tom interjected, ''why don't we get out of these hard chairs and eat our pie in the parlor?''

''Great idea,'' David returned.

Though she wasn't consulted on the matter, Alison, too, thought it was a good idea. Since David hadn't gotten around to showing her the room, she was curious to see it. She got up from her chair and followed the two men into the hallway.

The parlor didn't disappoint Alison. It was just as she'd envisioned it to be, a cozy space occupied by an overstuffed sofa and chair and assorted tables holding vases, lamps, and bric-a-brac. Bookshelves lined one wall from floor to ceiling; they were well supplied with books. In front of the sofa was a hearth fashioned of rough stone. Alison could picture the room warmed and lit by a roaring fire on a bitter cold night. A rug lay before the hearth.

Tom sat down in the chair and David settled himself on one end of the sofa. Huffy appeared suddenly in the room and curled himself up on the rug. Alison had no choice but to join David on the sofa. She seated herself on the other end.

While they ate their pie, Tom and David talked of the weather, David speculating whether there would even be color on the aspen this year.

"Those were the trees you showed me on the way to José's ranch," Alison commented to David.

"That's right. And, if it doesn't snow, you'll see what I meant about their beauty."

"Autumn is a beautiful time of year in Ohio, too."

"I'm sure it is, Alison. Most of the color around here comes from the cottonwood and aspen trees," David went on to explain.

"I like the fall," Tom put in. He looked reflective. "Sometime during your stay, Alison, you'll have to visit the Pueblo."

"Do you mean the Taos Pueblo?"

He nodded. "That's the one. Elizabeth went there once, by herself, to paint." Tom relaxed back in his chair, apparently ready to spin a story. "It was in the spring, if my memory serves me right."

Alison noted that David leaned forward, giving the older man his full attention. She did the same.

"Might have been April. Anyway, whatever month it was, the Pueblo Indians were having a big ceremonial dance. Feathers, headdresses, drums." He beat his hands against the arm of his chair in a fast, drumlike roll.

Alison giggled; David chuckled.

"Sounds like it was the perfect time for Elizabeth to do some painting," David offered. "Lots of action to capture at a powwow."

"Sure was." Tom shook his head. "But there was a tad too much action to suit her. Seems the Indians didn't take kindly to strangers making pictures of their sacred ceremonies. I respect that."

"What happened, Tom? Did they tell Elizabeth to leave?"

"Didn't tell her, Alison. I'm afraid they showed her instead."

"How do you mean?" David prompted.

"You see, she had her easel set up over to one side of

the grounds. The tribal chief must not have taken note of her until the ceremony was in full swing. But when he did, he took action real fast.'' Tom laughed softly at the memory. "I wasn't there, mind you. But I can see it as plain as anything. Elizabeth was up to her elbows in paint when the chief, in his full headdress, came along. Without as much as 'hello,' he picked up her easel and carried it off. Elizabeth went running behind him, trying to figure out what the heck was going on.''

Alison gave a gasp of surprise. "You mean that he kicked her out, just like that?''

Tom's eyes lit up merrily. "Kicked her out good and proper. Never did say as much as a word to her. But the chief got his message across, all the same. Elizabeth didn't visit the Pueblo after that. Embarrassed to, I reckon.''

Alison glanced at David. He was smiling at her. She smiled back, sensing the respect that David had for the older man. He'd likely heard Tom's stories on countless occasions, yet Alison imagined that he listened raptly, as if each retelling was the first time.

"I'll let you two in on a secret," Tom said in almost a whisper. Alison had to bend closer to hear. "There's nothing near as wonderful as being young and in love." He paused. "Unless it's being married and in love," he added with a wink at Alison.

Immediately, she averted her eyes from his gaze. No one spoke. Even David seemed rendered speechless by the remark. Desperate to change the subject, Alison said at last, "Tom, about your trip to Colorado that January. I'm dying to know what happened."

"You are, huh?" His face wore a satisfied expression. Then he suddenly stretched his arms above his head and gave an elaborate yawn. Slapping his leg, he said, "I'll be. I'm as sleepy as a bobcat after a big feed." He looked apologetically at Alison. "I'm sorry, but I'm afraid it's past my bedtime." Tom made a motion to get up from his chair.

Alison regarded Tom's actions with suspicion. A moment ago, he'd acted wide awake. She surmised his sudden sleepiness was contrived. Maybe he had the mistaken notion that she and David wanted to be alone. She appealed to him. "Tom, you're not going to put me off again, are you?"

"Afraid I am. But there's no need to get upset," he hastened to add. "David knows the story just as well as I do. Maybe better. I'm sure he wouldn't object to accommodating your curiosity, Alison." He turned to David. "Would you, now?"

David seemed to hesitate for an instant. "No, not at all," he replied. "But I doubt I can tell it with quite the same flourish as you."

"Go on," was Tom's response as he backed toward the door. "I'll be seeing you two tomorrow, I suppose," he said, leaving them alone with only a softly snoring dog for company.

Alison looked at David. He was watching her, a small smile curving his lips. There was an awkward pause, as if each was waiting for the other to speak. She did want to know the outcome of Tom and Elizabeth's escapade, but there was another tale she longed to hear first.

Drawing a breath, she said, "Do you remember when I told you that I like to nose around old graveyards?" It was an odd question, she knew, and David's response was a cocked eyebrow.

"I remember. Why? Do you imagine there's a cemetery buried in the snows of Trout Creek Pass?"

She laughed self-consciously. "No, but there's one I've taken an unusual interest in lately."

"The old Valera cemetery?"

"No. St. Ignacio's in Taos. And it's not so much the graveyard as it is a certain tombstone."

David shifted. He sat sideways on the sofa so that he was facing her. "Which tombstone, Alison?"

"It has an odd inscription on it, intriguing, really. It says 'Angel of Mora,' and that the person buried there is named Rosa Novato Chapman."

All at once David rose from the sofa and went to the hearth. His back to her, he said, "You think I can tell you something about the Angel of Mora?"

She sensed he might be able to tell her much, though she had no idea why he would possess such knowledge about a woman who'd died a very long time ago. "I was hoping you could," she said cautiously. "I doubt I'd have brought it up, but I mentioned my interest in the engraving to Rosella. She said you would be the best one to ask about the Angel."

David retraced the few steps to the sofa and sat down in the middle, very close to Alison.

She tried to retreat from him, but there was no place to retreat to. He didn't seem to notice. Clasping his hands together, he said, "Rosella said that, did she?"

Though he appeared at ease, Alison caught the guarded look in his eyes. *Like Rosella that day,* she recalled. But why? Was Rosa Chapman's story some somber secret not to be told? "Maybe Rosella was mistaken when she suggested I ask you. Maybe I shouldn't . . . "

David interrupted her with, "There's not very much to tell, Alison. I'm sorry." He shrugged, assuming a more relaxed posture. "The Angel of Mora is a local legend, one that . . . grew as people passed it down. Rosa Novato was a young Indian woman from the village of Mora. She fell in love with a white man named Chapman and married him, against her parents' warnings, and against Indian tradition."

"Why do I have a feeling this story won't have a happy ending?" Alison said softly. Even with the sparse details David had revealed, she felt a tingle of apprehension for Rosa Chapman's fate.

"Because it doesn't. But aren't most legends based on

tragedies?'' Without waiting for a response, David went on. ''Chapman was a bounty hunter, they say. One day in early autumn, he took off for the Sangre de Cristos in pursuit of a convicted murderer who'd escaped from a Texas prison. A mountain snowstorm came up suddenly. Fall storms are the most dangerous because they often catch people unprepared,'' he explained.

''Did he . . . did Chapman die in the storm?''

''He might have. His body was never found. But Rosa's was.''

Alison gasped, caught up in the tale. ''She was with him?''

''No. She had a baby at the time. But when Chapman didn't return, Rosa went looking for him. Alone.''

''How terrible.'' Alison saw that David's eyes gleamed in the waning sunlight that shone through the parlor's big west window. ''But why is she called the Angel of Mora?''

David appeared thoughtful. ''Because of her courage, her love for the man she'd married, the man she'd given up her heritage for. Those who knew Rosa well apparently decided it was a fitting title to bestow on her, an honor to her memory that would remain for others in the future to ponder over.''

''Others like me, you mean.'' Alison wanted to hear more, but David made no response. Was that all he knew of the story? Intuition told her it wasn't, but she didn't want to press him for details. ''I'm glad you shared the Angel's story with me, David.''

Silence fell between them and Alison became too aware of his nearness, too cognizant of the stillness enveloping the old house now that Tom had gone off to bed. She got up from the sofa and made a show of checking her watch.

''I didn't realize how late it's getting,'' she said, glancing at David. ''I need to do some work in my studio tonight.'' He gave no reply to this. She remembered the empty dessert bowl that she still held in her hand. ''Would you . . . could you tell me where the kitchen is so that I can drop this off?''

David stood up beside her. ''I'll drop it off for you.'' Before she could protest, he reached for the bowl. His fingers made contact with hers. The next thing she knew, he'd set down the bowl and taken her hand in his.

''Do you have to go?'' he asked with obvious disappointment. ''I thought you were so eager to hear the saga of Trout Creek Pass.''

The small attempt at humor drew a brief smile from Alison. But most of her attention was focused on the feel of his hand surrounding hers. ''I was. That is, I am, but I made a schedule for myself, you see, and it's important that . . . '' Her words died as David moved closer. His hand let go of hers to slip around her waist. He held her loosely; she could easily have gotten away—if she had wanted to.

To her frustration, Alison found that she didn't want to. Instead, she tilted her head up in expectation of the kiss she sensed was coming, the one he had almost given her in the Jeep. Their lips came together gently. There was no awkwardness at all and it seemed the most natural thing in the world that David should be kissing her.

When it ended, his lips brushed her brow, and she leaned against him, giving in to a feeling she hadn't known in a very long time.

Then vaguely she became aware that David was moving her slowly back from himself. His eyes, darkly veiled, held hers. ''Good luck with your painting,'' he whispered.

Heat flooded Alison's cheeks. She opened her mouth, but nothing came out. Why had he done this to her? Why had she allowed it? She desperately tried to compose herself and failed.

There was nothing to do but tear herself from his arms and hurry from the room. As she went, it registered somewhere in her mind that David didn't call to her. He didn't try to stop her from going.

Chapter Seven

Alison stepped back from her easel and studied the portrait of Tom and Nubbins that she had just completed. It had turned out well. Her trained eye picked out only a couple of places that needed a bit of touching up.

She decided she would invite Tom to come back to her studio to view the portrait after dinner the next evening. She imagined what his reaction might be, and it brought a smile to her face.

Another thing that brought a smile to Alison's face was the fact that she had not only finished the portrait, but the mountain scene as well. And she had David to credit for her extreme diligence and productivity over the weekend. For the kiss they had shared in the privacy of the parlor, her flustered flight from him afterward, had served to fuel her creativity in a manner she would never have thought possible.

The emotions David's nearness had stirred in her forced her to sternly remind herself of the reason why she was

76

here in this spacious old home, why she had come to New Mexico in the first place. She wasn't in Taos to fall head over paintbrush for an admittedly handsome and witty veterinarian whose kiss just happened to have the most unsettling effect on her.

The smile faded, turned into a stubborn frown. She'd already vowed not to let David kiss her again. And her determination had brought her a certain peace of mind. Then why did her completion of the two paintings seem a hollow victory?

Sighing, Alison set about cleaning up her studio. She set herself to the task, purposely keeping her back turned to the window that looked out on David's *casa*. Suddenly the small room seemed too confining to her, almost claustrophobic. Alison realized the size of the room wasn't the problem. She had plenty of space in which to do her painting.

Instead, she knew her feelings were more due to the fact she'd spent too much time in her studio the past few days. She would soon remedy that, she thought as she laid her brushes aside on the counter and stored her palette in the cabinet.

The next morning she would go downtown and buy the supplies she planned to surprise Miguel with on her next trip to Valera. Maybe she would visit a few of the galleries that lined the plaza, though she had made up her mind before leaving Cincinnati that she wasn't going to spend a lot of time viewing the works of Taos's local artisans. She secretly feared she'd be intimidated by their quality.

Another idea occurred to her. If she had time before noon, she would stop by St. Ignacio's and make the tracing of Rosa Chapman's grave that she'd wanted to do. A tingle of anticipation went through Alison as she recalled the Angel's tale. But was it the legend itself that set her nerves slightly on edge? Or was it more the memory of the one who had related the story?

*   *   *

"That will be forty-two dollars and sixty-seven cents, please."

Alison began to count out bills from her purse, handing them to the clerk on the other side of the counter. She had bought more than she'd intended to at the well-stocked art supply store she had discovered on one corner of the plaza. Besides the couple of paintbrushes, palette, and small easel she had chosen for Miguel, she'd found a sable brush to replace one in her set that had begun to shed its bristles.

"All right, there you are," the clerk said as he handed her change for the five tens she had given him. He smiled at her.

The gray-haired man, whom Alison estimated to be in his fifties, had been pleasant and helpful, showing her where the various supplies were stocked on the shelves. They'd conversed a little as she shopped.

Now she thought he might be able to answer another question for her. "I've noticed there seem to be a great number of galleries in town. Are there any you would particularly recommend?"

"Solaria," he responded without hesitation. "In my opinion, it's the finest gallery in Taos. The only thing is, it's located a few blocks up from the plaza on Romero Street. Solaria's a favorite with the local patrons, but some folks passing through miss it, and that's a shame." His mouth turned down at the corners for an instant. Then the smile was back in place. "On the plaza, I'd suggest you check out the Four Winds Gallery and Mountain Thunder Artisans. They showcase the works of Taos's best artists." He gave her directions to both.

"I'll check out all of them," Alison said as she gathered her parcels from off the counter. "And thank you for your help."

"Come back again," the man said.

"I will," she replied as she headed for the door.

Outside the store there was a heavy flow of pedestrian traffic. Alison looked around, trying to make up her mind whether to walk the few blocks to Solaria or wait for another day. She consulted her watch. It was already ten-thirty. If she wanted to grab a sandwich for lunch and get back to her studio for the afternoon, she would hardly be able to do Solaria justice. She opted to make a quick tour of Four Winds and Mountain Thunder Artisans.

To her disappointment, the two galleries were so crowded she could barely inch her way through the exhibits. She did get a glimpse or two of most of the paintings and sculptures on display. Many carried a Southwestern theme, featuring either mountain scenes not unlike the one she'd just painted or aspects of Pueblo Indian life. She was impressed by the variety of media employed. There were bright and bold oils, pale and serene watercolors, a fair number of lovely gouache renderings, and charcoal and pen-and-ink drawings.

But the crush of people constantly dodging and jockeying past her made for a frustrating experience. Alison left the galleries and the downtown plaza with the idea of returning after tourist season slowed in Taos.

Her stomach gave a rumble. Apparently the neglect of having no more than a granola bar for breakfast had caught up with her. The hoped-for stop at St. Ignacio's would have to wait for another morning, too, in favor of food.

As she headed for the outdoor café where she'd enjoyed lunch before, Alison thought of the beautiful woman who had caused such a stir among the diners. Would Delphinia Rios make a grand entrance again today? If she did, would it be on the arm of her "handsome young man" as Amelia had described him? The notion brought a smile to Alison's lips.

"I'll be. Do I really look like that?" Tom stood, hands behind his back, staring at his portrait.

From the happy expression he wore, Alison took the question as a compliment. "I hope I did you justice, Tom," she said, afraid that she sounded as if she were fishing for praise.

He brought his hand up and smoothed back his white hair. "You did me a lot of justice, I'd say. And Nubbins, well . . . " Tom shook his head. "You got him about perfect, taking that walnut from my hand like he always does."

"I'm hoping to feature the painting in Paul's show." She had told Tom about Paul over dinner one evening.

Tom fairly beamed. "You mean a lot of people dressed up in fancy clothes will be taking a gander at me and Nubbins?"

"That's right. In fact . . . " A knock at the door interrupted Alison. Her heart gave a little leap. "Come in," she said, wondering if it were Lucy on the other side of the door instead of the person she imagined was there.

The door swung back, and David stepped cautiously into the room. He glanced around before his gaze settled on her. "I hope I'm not interrupting you."

She'd imagined right. "No, not at all, David. I was showing Tom his portrait."

David regarded Tom as if he'd just now noticed the older man's presence.

"And a mighty fine job Alison did on it too," Tom declared.

David came forward to where Alison and Tom stood in front of the easel. He studied the canvas that was set on the easel. "You're right, Tom," he agreed. Addressing Alison, he said, "You did do a mighty fine job." But his eyes told her more than that.

Warmth flooded her face as the memory of his kiss stubbornly occupied her mind. "Thank you," she managed, turning her head from him. *This is ridiculous,* she chided herself. *The man kisses you once and you act like a school-girl with a mad crush.*

Dimly, she heard Tom talking to David. Her ears picked up snatches of the conversation. Something about David missing a good dinner, and when was he going to start keeping sensible hours at that clinic of his. Then, ''Well, I'd best be going.''

Alison came to attention. She wasn't about to let Tom get away so easily this time. ''Don't be in a hurry, Tom. I have a gift for you.''

His eyebrows arched inquisitively, and to Alison's relief, he stayed put where he was.

She went to the cabinet, retrieved the sheet of paper she'd stashed there earlier, and returned with it. ''Here,'' she said, handing the sheet to Tom.

''Why . . . it's the very same picture of me and Nubbins that you painted, only this one's not colored over.''

''That's the pencil sketch I used as a pattern for the painting. The drawing was pretty rough. I touched it up a bit because I wanted you to have it.'' In reality, she had not intended to give it to Tom so soon. But David's sudden appearance at the studio, the effect he had on her, had caused her to act in haste. Yet she couldn't regret presenting Tom with the drawing—not when he appeared so pleased about it.

''Ah,'' he said at last, ''you shouldn't have gone to the trouble.''

''Not any trouble at all, just my way of thanking you for posing for me.''

He gave her a big grin. ''You know what I'm going to do? I'm going to set this up in my room, and I've got a nice frame that should just about fit around it.''

''That's a terrific idea, Tom.'' This came from David.

Tom turned abruptly on his heel and headed for the door. Pausing on the threshold, he raised his hand in a wave to Alison, then left, whistling under his breath.

Tom, you've done it again, Alison thought as she watched his retreat. When she dared to look at David, she suddenly remembered the supplies she'd bought for Miguel. "There's something I want to show you, too." She led him over to the counter where the brushes, palette, and folded easel were piled. "These are for Miguel."

David picked up the palette and examined it. "Nice," he commented, wriggling his thumb through the hole in the board. It was a tight fit.

Alison had to smile. "I wanted Miguel to have the right size palette for his small hand. I plan to give him a few tubes of my own paint. I brought extra along."

"As if there weren't any to be bought in Taos," David remarked.

She took the comment in the teasing way that he obviously meant it. "I've been known to be . . . overenthusiastic in my packing."

David chuckled. "I can tell you this much. You're going to have one overenthusiastic little boy on your hands next Tuesday."

"Is that why you stopped by, to remind me of Miguel's first lesson?" Alison considered that David was standing too close.

"No. I don't think you'd forget an appointment as important as that. But I did want to let you know I spoke with Paul Suarez and he was more than happy to give Miguel time off from school for private art lessons." David removed his thumb from the hole and laid the palette on the counter. "Another reason I came by is because I was curious as to how this room's working out for you."

"It's working out great. It's so quiet, like you said, and I've been very productive. Look." She went to get the other painting from where she'd left it to dry. She held it up for David's inspection.

He stared at the canvas for a moment.

"You recognize the scene, don't you?"

"Of course. But how did you happen to shade the slopes of the mountains like that? It's the color they take on at sunrise," he said in amazement.

She wondered how many mornings he had seen the sun come up over that particular part of the Sangre de Cristo range. Had he enjoyed the spectacle alone—or with a companion? "A certain overenthusiastic little boy advised me, David."

David's eyes crinkled with humor as they captured hers above the painting. Then he grew serious. "You're a very talented artist, Alison. And I'm not saying that to flatter you."

But she was flattered, though she knew David meant the compliment sincerely. "I'm trying to work at developing what Paul calls my 'potential.' I hope I'll be successful during my stay here."

"I think you already are." He hesitated. "I'm sorry. I have to be somewhere in about forty-five minutes and I've got to eat and change my clothes first."

Why should he apologize for leaving when he had only dropped by to begin with? "You don't have to be sorry. I mean, you just stopped for a minute, but now you've got an appointment and you have to leave." Or was it a *date* instead?

"Yes, I have to leave." David turned away from her.

Had she sounded eager to be rid of him? Or was he only mimicking her own hasty departure from the parlor that evening not long ago? "I'm glad you came by, David."

He rewarded her with a half smile and an equally trite reply. "I'm glad you showed me your paintings, Alison."

With that, he was gone. Alison watched after his retreating shadow. To her annoyance, she had briefly wondered if he might take her in his arms and kiss her again. But he had given no indication that the romantic interlude they had shared held any place of importance in his thoughts.

Even as she renewed her determination to put any romantic ideas of David Grier from her mind, she couldn't deny that a certain chemistry existed between them. Yet he must be used to that too. No doubt he was accustomed to receiving plenty of attention from women—beautiful women, to be exact. Perhaps the kisses he had given her had been enough to satisfy his curiosity about her.

He might even have a steady girlfriend, contrary to Tom's belief. Or he might play the field. Alison could see David as one of the town's most eligible bachelors. Somehow that made her feel both relieved and wretched.

As she put out the light in her studio and prepared to go upstairs to the loft, she told herself she was being absurd. She was not about to get involved with David Grier, and whether he dated one woman or twenty was of no concern to her at all.

Tuesday morning dawned brilliant and clear, the sky a flawless azure blue. It was ideal weather for a trip to Valera, Alison thought as she hurried to collect the last of her supplies and stuff them into her knapsack.

She wasn't late. David had told her the evening before that she should be ready to leave at eight o'clock. It was seven-fifty now. But on her way down the steps from the loft she'd heard barking, and when she looked out the window by the door, she had spotted Huffy racing across the length of the yard. Then she'd seen David hefting his equipment case into the Jeep which was parked in the driveway by the house.

She'd concluded he must be anxious to start off and she had no wish to keep him waiting. She slung her knapsack over her free arm and shoulder. In her other arm she carried a jacket and Miguel's easel. With a sense of expectation, Alison walked down the hall and out the front door to the Jeep.

She greeted David and reached back to give Huffy a pat

before climbing into the passenger seat. Huffy let out an excited bark in return.

"I see that Lucy got to you this morning," David said with a grin.

"You mean the jacket?" Alison grinned back. "Well, yes, she suggested that I might need it. But I don't think so." Settling in the seat, she tilted her face up to receive the benevolent warmth of the sun. There wasn't a cloud in sight. Summer seemed firmly ensconced still.

"Lucy's right. My jacket's in the boot with Huffy." With that comment, David started the Jeep and let it roll down the driveway.

Alison regarded him. He wore jeans and a short-sleeved white shirt that showed off his tan in a striking way. "You think the weather's going to turn? It's so beautiful now."

"Remember when I said fall snowstorms are the most dangerous?"

"Yes." How could she forget? He had been telling the Angel of Mora's tale at the time.

He downshifted the Jeep as it swung out onto the street. The vehicle whined, shuddered with the changing of gears, then moved forward. "Actually, they're forecasting snow for just the mountains, but I can feel it in the air even down here."

"You can?" Alison couldn't help sounding skeptical. Yet David was from the area; she was forced to respect his opinion.

"Didn't you notice? That touch of briskness?" He glanced quizzically at her.

She raised her face again to the air. There was a breeze; it caressed her cheeks. No chill. "I'm sorry. I guess it takes a native to know the vagaries of the local climate."

David just chuckled. He seemed in a good mood and Alison's own spirits were heightened. She had a feeling this was going to be a memorable day. Last night in the quiet darkness of the loft, she had put to rest the matter of the kiss, what it had meant and hadn't meant. She had resolved to view David as no more, or less, than a casual friend for the duration of her stay in Taos.

As they left town behind and headed into the mountains, Alison thought about the prediction of snow, thought about winter, which for the moment seemed far away. "Isn't Taos a popular ski area in the winter?" she asked David.

"Sure is. It's almost as well known for its ski resorts as it is for its galleries."

"Do you ski?"

David glanced her way. "I used to. In fact, for a while I was a regular ski bum."

That was somehow hard for her to imagine, though she could envision him on a pair of skis plunging down some snowy hill. "But you gave it up?"

"Not exactly. I still enjoy a good run on the slopes at Angel Fire. That's one of our local resorts," he explained. "I did get away from skiing while I was in California. Instead of bundling up for a cold day on skis, when I had a little free time, I put on my bathing trunks and headed for the beach."

"I have to admit that sounds more appealing."

David laughed. "I take it you don't care for winter sports."

"I've been cross-country skiing and I liked that."

"Cross-country is my favorite," he put in. "But what I enjoy even more is hiking."

"So do I."

He smiled across at her, then gave his attention back to the road ahead. "There's nothing like it. To find a spot somewhere, just be alone, maybe beside a stream where you can listen to the water and watch the clouds roll by. A place where it's peaceful and you can sit and think or skip a few stones."

"You like to skip stones? I can't believe it." Why this small revelation delighted her so, Alison wasn't sure. But it opened up a whole topic of conversation. She told him about Laurel Gorge, the times she'd gone there by herself, or with a few friends from the Institute, to walk the trails, to contemplate, to sketch, to skip stones.

She asked David about his own favorite places to hike, and he revealed that he and Martin used to go often in the summer, choosing a different route each time that they had mapped out beforehand. As he described to her some of the sights he had seen on the outings, Alison saw them in her mind.

"Where is Martin now?" she said when David had finished.

"In Fort Worth. He's a guidance counselor at one of the high schools there, has a wife and three kids. I haven't seen him in a while. But he and his family will be coming home for a visit in December."

Alison observed David. His profile gave nothing away, but there'd been a touch of wistfulness in his voice when he spoke of Martin. Perhaps he was thinking of Eileen as well, of how, like Martin, he might have a family of his own if he and Eileen had married.

Absorbed in her conversation with David, and absorbed in her own thoughts, Alison had barely noticed the subtle, but definite, shift in the weather. Now it was impossible to ignore.

There was a biting edge to the air that forced her to roll up her partially opened window. David tossed her a smile and cranked up his window too. She took the smile as a friendly, if mute, "I told you so."

And there were the clouds, puffy and billowing, where only clear sky had been before. They scudded across the heavens, chased by a rising wind.

As they approached the turnoff for the dirt road that led to Valera, Alison gazed at the ridge of mountaintops. In her painting, she had washed their slopes in shades of lavender and pink and gold. But today the mountains had taken on an ominous appearance, and a bank of dreary gray clouds shrouded the spiny peaks. Those clouds looked like they carried snow. They looked like winter.

A shiver went through Alison. She reached for her jacket and put it on. In the back, Huffy stirred and let out a little yap as if to protest the change in the weather. But David made no comment.

Chapter Eight

Miguel was waiting for Alison and David outside the community center. He waved and ran, as fast as his legs would allow, toward the Jeep as David brought it to a stop.

Alison noted with some small alarm that the boy wore no coat, only a thin, ragged-looking shirt and patched jeans. Miguel didn't seem to mind the cold, however. Clutching a sheaf of papers in his hand, he called, "Hi, Miss Hughes! I brought some of my pictures for you to see." Then, before she could respond, he was off to the other side of the Jeep to greet David as he climbed out.

He followed them to the back of the vehicle, where David handed him a leather instrument bag to carry. Alison gathered her knapsack and slipped the folded easel under her arm, concealing it as best she could from any inquiring eyes.

"Let me," David offered in a whisper. He lifted the easel from her hands, wrapped it deftly in his jacket, and headed for the door of the community center.

Miguel led the way and Alison felt a certain satisfaction in knowing the youngster had already lost a good measure of the shyness he'd initially displayed towards her.

A bitter gust of wind came out of nowhere, whipping around the corner of the building. Alison was glad for her jacket, glad too for the warm blast of air that hit her cheeks as Miguel held the door open for her.

Rosella met them inside the big main room. There was an older woman with her whom Alison didn't recognize. Had she met the woman before?

She hadn't. Rosella introduced the woman as Carmen Montez.

For a moment, the four adults discussed among themselves the sudden change in the weather. Carmen's eyes narrowed in her wizened face as her gaze settled on Alison "*Sí*, the September storms are the most deadly," she said with a heavy sigh. Her frail shoulders sagged. "Foolish souls can lose their way in the mountains. They are not found until spring. Then it is too late. Sometimes," she continued in a whispery voice, "they are never found."

The pronouncement chilled Alison, despite the cozy environs of the center. She immediately thought of the Angel of Mora. *Chapman's body was never found. But Rosa's was.* She glanced at David. His face wore a serious expression. Could he be thinking of the Angel too? His eyes caught hers.

No one spoke for a time. Then Miguel, no doubt impatient to get on with the day's activities, said, "Miss Hughes, we're going to use the room down the hall for our lesson. Rosella told me we could."

"That's fine," she responded, though David still commanded her attention.

"Just give me a second to lay out my instruments," David said, "and I'll help you two get set up."

"And I'll help *you*, Dr. Dave." With solemn pride, Miguel toted the instrument bag over to a large table along the far wall. A folding screen stood nearby. Alison deduced that, with the screen placed in front of it, the table served as David's "clinic."

Rosella excused herself, telling Alison she would see her at lunch. Carmen gave Alison a nod and left too.

In a short time David and Miguel were back. "Shall we give Miss Hughes a tour of the center first?" David asked his young assistant.

"Sure!" Miguel's eyes lit up at the prospect. He motioned for Alison to follow him.

Alison was impressed by what she saw, even more so for having learned that the building had been a labor of love. Just off the main room there was a large well-equipped kitchen. From the kitchen a corridor led to the bathrooms, and at the end of the corridor was the room Miguel had spoken of.

The room had a window that looked out on the mountains. There were shelves with books and games and puzzles stacked on them. There was a table and a countertop and even a double sink with faucets.

"The room's perfect," Alison declared. "And I'm very impressed with your community center, Miguel. Did you help build it?"

"Uh-huh. I got to carry some boards and watch the toolbox. That was so nobody would take anything they weren't supposed to," he explained proudly. "I even got to hammer nails sometimes."

"Well, all of you did a wonderful job." Miguel flashed a shy smile at Alison's compliment.

"Now it's time to learn to use a paintbrush," David declared. He passed the jacket-shrouded easel to Alison and moved to leave.

She held him with her hand and the plea, "Can you spare one more minute?" For some reason, she wanted David to be there when she gave Miguel his present.

"Two, if you want, Alison," he replied softly. She smiled in response.

Unzipping her knapsack, she pulled out the palette, brushes, and tubes of paint. "Like Dr. Dave said, Miguel, we'll be learning to paint, and to do that, we need special tools, just like you did when you built the community center. So I brought you these, to help you get started." She laid out the supplies on the table.

"For me?" The boy's eyes grew big as he stepped closer.

"Yes. And also this." She unwrapped the easel and set it in front of Miguel.

"Wow! Neat!" Still holding his pictures, he reached out with one hand and touched the wooden frame of the easel, touched the palette and brushes too, as if the small act made the gift truly his. "Thank you, Miss Hughes," he said in a hushed voice, though his face was positively beaming.

Over Miguel's head, Alison met David's eyes. They signaled his gratitude for her thoughtfulness. Yet it wasn't the act of giving Miguel the few supplies that was of primary importance to her. Her true test would come in how well she was able to teach Miguel to use those vital tools of an artist's trade.

From the other end of the hall came a bleating sound. "It seems you've got a patient waiting."

"Yes, Alison, I believe you're right." But it took another, more insistent cry from the same distressed animal to set David in motion. At the door, he called back, "You two have a good lesson." To Alison in particular, he said, "I'll see you at lunch."

She waited, heard David's footsteps echoing down the corridor. Then she turned to Miguel. "First," she said, putting her arm lightly around the boy's shoulders, "why don't you show me the drawings you've brought."

They went through his pictures, one by one. There were drawings of mountains, animals, trees, a house which Miguel explained was his, as well as portraits of various villagers. Alison immediately recognized the one of Ruben.

"Which picture would you most like to make a painting of?" she asked after they'd gone through them. She wasn't surprised when Miguel picked the drawing of Skeezer that he'd first shown her.

Alison explained that artists often used sketches, like those he'd done, as a pattern for their paintings.

"What do you suppose we should do to begin, Miguel?" she said, tacking a piece of blank paper to a board she'd brought along. She positioned the board on the easel.

Miguel rubbed his chin thoughtfully. "Paint Skeezer?"

Alison smiled. "Well, yes, we'll be doing that. But first we need to learn our colors and how to mix them. Also how to use our brushes properly. An excellent way to learn is to practice painting something simple. Can you think of anything that would be easy to paint?"

Miguel considered the question as before. "How about a sky?" He looked out the window and frowned. "But not yucky like today. A *blue* sky."

Alison hid a smile. "That's a great idea. I couldn't have thought of a better one myself." She picked up a tube of paint.

"This color is Cerulean blue," she said, squeezing a dollop of the paint onto Miguel's palette. "And this one," she went on, "is Chinese white." She put a bit of it near the blue on the palette. "We can practice mixing them together. No white or only a little and we'll have a darker sky. A lot of white mixed in with the blue and we'll have . . . "

"A lighter sky," Miguel offered eagerly.

Alison found the boy's enthusiasm irresistible, but a small caution was in order. "You know, Miguel, painting a sky should be fun. But some of the techniques we'll be learning may take a little longer. We might have to work very hard. We'll need to have patience and keep trying, even if we find we need to practice some things over and over."

"I don't mind practicing, Miss Hughes. And I'll work hard because I want to be a good artist someday. Like you," he added shyly.

Alison put her hand on Miguel's shoulder. "I'm positive you can be even better than good. So why don't we start then by mixing our Cerulean blue with a little water and the white and see what kind of a sky we can come up with?"

A call came in for David from José Flores just as lunch was over.

"José's mare is having problems," David said on returning to the table where Alison sat waiting. "This time, I'm afraid, it's not a false alarm. We'll need to leave right away."

Alison immediately rose from the table. "Is it the foal?"

"Yes. The mare's been in labor for some time and things aren't progressing as they should. I won't know exactly what's going on until I get there." David shrugged into his jacket and motioned for Rosella, who was standing a short distance away. She came over to him. David apprised her of the situation and asked if she would let his other appointments know that he might not make it today.

"Don't worry. I'll take care of everything," she said and quickly left.

"The other calls weren't all that urgent," he said to Alison as she grabbed her knapsack and followed him from the center.

She was glad she had thought to pack up her ever-present sketchbook and other supplies before lunch. Miguel had gone home to eat and be taken to school by his aunt. With Rosella's approval, his easel and other equipment had been stashed on a shelf in the back room of the center. He could return any time the center was open to work on the lesson Alison had given him.

Alison thought that it was a considerate arrangement—not unlike the one David had made for her. Over an almost leisurely meal, she had told David of the morning's progress, of the first assignment she had given Miguel to practice mixing primary colors with each other and with Chinese white to create new colors. With the new shades, he was to try painting easy things, like grass, a blue sky with clouds, a tree. She'd promised him that on her next trip they would start the portrait of Skeezer.

David had listened with great interest and then told her of his own experiences that morning. But now, with the urgent call from José, Alison took up worrying about the expectant mare and her foal—not to mention the steadily deteriorating weather.

She remembered the tortuous route that led to José's ranch. From what she'd seen out the window of the community center, Valera had so far received only a dusting of snow. She was sure conditions would be worse farther up, where José lived.

They were worse. As the Jeep climbed higher, the snow grew heavier, the wind fiercer than at Valera. A goodly amount of snow had accumulated on the ground and lay as slush on the road. But the vehicle hugged the road easily, never veering or fishtailing as David guided it around the hairpin curves. Alison could understand why he'd chosen a Jeep to get around in the mountains.

When they arrived at the ranch, José was in the yard, waiting. David got out immediately, snatched his instrument bag from the boot, and headed for the barn. Huffy jumped down from the spot where he'd been curled up in the back, bounding onto the snow-covered ground after David.

Alison wasn't certain what to do, except that she knew she was not going to accompany David to the barn. She couldn't bear the idea of having to watch the mare in agony, trying to give birth to her foal. Nor did she think her presence there would be welcome.

José stepped up and in an instant solved Alison's dilemma. "Please," he said, gesturing for her to get out of the Jeep, "you must go inside the house. It's much too cold for you to stay here."

"I'm very sorry about your mare," she said, longing to show her concern, yet knowing nothing she might say could ease the rancher's anxiety.

"Dr. Dave will be able to help," José said with astonishing certainty. "Now come with me."

She got her knapsack from off the floor where she'd put it and went with him.

José led her into the kitchen of his small home. The room was almost dark, with only a small window over the sink. Everything was quiet except for the ticking of a clock above the refrigerator. It was obvious no one else was about, and from the austere, homely furnishings, Alison guessed that José was a bachelor. She wondered if he didn't get lonely living in such an isolated spot high in the Sangre de Cristos.

He indicated for her to have a seat in a rocking chair that had been placed in a corner of the kitchen. Beside the chair was a wood-burning stove. A fire crackled in the stove, lending warmth to the room.

"Would you like a cup of coffee, Alison?" he asked. Not waiting for an answer, he poured her one from a blue porcelain pot that stood on a burner of his range. "Cream or sugar?" he asked, handing her the steaming cup.

"I like it black. Thank you." She wrapped her fingers around the mug, only then realizing how cold and numb her hands were.

José switched on a lamp that was bracketed to the wall. The illumination brightened the gloomy kitchen. "Will you be all right?" he asked.

"Fine." Alison felt strangely pampered. It touched her heart that this man who had a pregnant mare in dire straits would show her such attention.

"I must go," he said. He started off, then stopped at the door. "The bathroom's just through the living room," he told her, "and please help yourself to more coffee. It may be a while."

There was one favor she had to ask of him. "José, I wonder if . . . could you or David let me know when everything's okay?"

He gave her a brief smile. "We will," he said, and was off, shutting the door behind him before the wind could blow any snow in.

Alison sat for a few minutes, sipping her coffee. The brew was strong and rich and scalding, just the way she liked it. After her fingers felt thawed out, she reached for her knapsack and took out her sketchbook and a pencil. She was bound to be concerned for the welfare of the mare and foal, but she also saw an opportunity to do a bit of work on her own projects. She opened the book and leafed through the drawings she had made of St. Ignacio's cemetery and the Angel of Mora's gravestone. She'd already decided to do a watercolor rendition of the gravestone with its intriguing inscription and thick green grass growing up around it.

Now she would more carefully study the other sketches of the yard to see if any of them showed particular promise. She considered them one by one, stopping to pencil in certain details that she'd originally left out, but recalled in her mind. Other details she added from her imagination. In between, she drank coffee, emptying the mug and refilling it twice from the porcelain pot.

Involved in her work, Alison soon lost track of time. She was startled when, at last, she heard a sound other than the ticking of the clock and the intermittent howling of the wind.

The kitchen door creaked open and David came in. He stomped and wiped his snow-covered shoes on a mat that lay by the door. "I'm afraid Lucy should have warned us to bring our boots too," he said, crossing the room to where Alison sat in the rocker.

She rose immediately, putting aside her sketchbook. "How is the mare?" she asked, not sure she wanted to know.

David ran his hand through his hair; loosened bits of snow fell onto his jacket. "She'll be all right. The foal, too."

"Thank goodness." Alison felt slightly weak. She must have been more worried than she'd realized. "What was wrong?" Absently, she picked up her coffee mug and took a swallow.

"Do you honestly want to know?"

"I think I do."

David gave a small laugh. "Well, one of the foal's fore-legs was bent backward. It couldn't go through the birth canal that way. It took me a while, but I finally fixed the problem."

"I see." Alison had no wish to ask how he had "fixed the problem."

"I take it you've been comfortable in here?"

"Very." She returned David's smile. "José's a kind man."

"Yes, he is." David regarded her closely. "I wonder if you might want to leave the warmth and your coffee for a few minutes and see something miraculous. The birth of the foal. It's about to happen."

Alison's hands tightened reflexively around the mug. "I . . . I have to tell you I've never seen anything like that before."

"Would you like to? You can come back to the house if you find the experience too traumatic."

Suddenly she realized that she did want to see the birth,

more than she could have imagined. And David had graciously given her an out—just in case. "Let me put my jacket on."

David helped her with the jacket. Then he took hold of her arm and led her through the drifting snow to the barn.

Inside, the structure was surprisingly warm. Not like the kitchen, Alison thought, but secure from the elements.

Then Alison saw the mare. She was moving in an ungainly way across the straw-covered floor at the end of the barn. David whispered, "Right about here," and guided Alison to a stop a good distance away, yet near enough to get a clear view of the unfolding drama. José came to stand on the other side of David.

Without warning, the mare nickered and fell into a heap on the floor. She began to roll from side to side, as if she had convulsions.

"Don't worry. That's normal." David's voice was very close to Alison's ear.

She turned to him. His face wore a look of satisfaction. She understood. He had been able to help the mare, had undoubtedly saved both her life and the foal's. Could there be any greater source of contentment than that? Very briefly, Alison considered that the joy she knew on completion of a painting must pale in comparison to David's happiness just now, not to mention José's.

Her attention was soon drawn back to the mare. The animal had gotten up again and was now kicking at her swollen belly, perhaps to tell the foal that it was time to be on its way out into the world.

And, as if the foal had gotten the message, a foot appeared from the mare's birth canal. Alison blinked, not sure she'd seen right. But there was no mistake. The foot was swiftly followed by the leg it was attached to. Then things happened so fast Alison couldn't be certain afterwards that she had witnessed it all.

The mare collapsed onto the floor again and the tiny foal

slid out into the world. Whole. Complete. Perfect, from all appearances.

"Oh," Alison breathed. Her hands flew to her face. Her eyes went misty. "It is a miracle."

"See. That wasn't so bad, was it?" David said quietly. But before she could respond, he had left her side to attend to the new foal and its mother.

José followed David and, together, the two men inspected the newborn animal. "You've got a fine, healthy colt," she heard David say.

José took hold of David's hand, pumping it in a hearty handshake.

Then, while David went around to examine the mare, Alison watched the foal's valiant attempts to struggle to his feet. But his efforts proved futile, as he tried to hoist himself up on the frailest-looking of legs. At last the foal's persistence met with success as he stood and took a couple of wobbly steps toward his mother. Though he nearly toppled over once more, he kept on, tottering forward with a measure of shaky determination.

In turn, the mare nudged her infant. The foal discovered what he was searching for and vigorously set about getting his first meal. Alison smiled, but her eyes went watery again.

José brought a bucket and large towel. David washed his hands and arms in the soapy water and dried them on the towel. Then he and José came back to where Alison stood.

It was at this point that Alison noticed Huffy. He must have been sleeping in one of the heaps of straw strewn around the barn. Wagging his tail, he nuzzled his face against David's hand and gave a soft whimper as if to ask, "Have I missed out on something?" Wisps of straw clung to his long silky hair.

"Won't you come in to the house for a little while?" José asked after a moment. "You can get warm, have coffee and doughnuts. I bought the doughnuts just this morning at the Minute Mart.''

Alison noted that José's face no longer wore an anxious expression. He looked relaxed.

David consulted his watch. ''Maybe just a quick cup of coffee, unless Alison's hungry.'' He looked at her inquiringly.

''Not especially.'' It wasn't a lie. She hadn't even thought about food.

''With the weather, we'd better be heading back down the mountain. It'll take a while to get home.''

''Of course,'' José agreed. He led the way out of the barn. A rush of cold air and stinging snow met their faces.

They hurried across the yard and into the sanctuary of José's kitchen. As Alison watched him pour David a mug of coffee, she had an idea.

José reached for the mug she had used. She stopped him before he could fill it. ''The coffee's delicious, José, but I had three cups and that was plenty. I was wondering though,'' she continued, turning to David, ''if while you're drinking yours, I might go and make a fast drawing of the mare and her new colt?''

David eyed her in a contented way over the top of his mug. ''I think that would be a terrific idea.''

She grabbed her sketchbook and ran back through the snow to the barn. Inside, all was quiet except for the lusty sound of the foal nursing and the soft, contented neighing of its mother.

Alison made her sketch, knowing she could flesh out the scene later when she had a chance. Soon David and José came, and David asked if she was ready to leave.

José accompanied them to the Jeep, but he didn't linger long in the bitter weather. After a promise from David to check in by phone the next day, José raised his hand in a wave and headed for the refuge of his home.

David started the Jeep and let it idle for a minute. He looked over at Alison. "Are you apprehensive?"

"Apprehensive?" At first, she didn't know what he meant.

He smiled. "I mean about the trip down. The roads won't be in good shape. I doubt any plows have been out."

She considered the matter. It was true that traveling high mountain roads—in particular, snow-covered mountain roads—wasn't her favorite activity. Her gaze fell on David's hands where they rested lightly on the steering wheel. She was reminded of their strength, their warmth, the way they had gently held her own. She had no doubt that those hands were just as capable of safely steering the Jeep down a slippery high country road as they were of helping a vulnerable foal find its way into the world.

"No, I'm not afraid," she said at last. "Not in the least."

"I'm glad," David said. Still, he didn't move to set the Jeep in motion. "And you know what? Despite the weather, I think the events of the day call for a minor celebration. Don't you?"

Again, Alison was taken off guard. "A . . . celebration? Oh . . . you mean the new foal." She must sound hopelessly dense.

"I do. Since there's no way we'll be home in time for dinner, I thought we might . . . "

"Have a Mesquite Burger," she finished for him. "So what you're trying to say is you're hungry for one of Sheldon's specials."

David shook his head. "No, that's not what I'm trying to say. I believe what I'm trying to say is, would you have dinner with me tonight? Not a Mesquite Burger or any other kind of burger. A real meal. Steak. And lobster tail. And wine." He gazed at her expectantly.

"Steak. Lobster tail. Wine," she echoed.

"At Bolero's in Taos," he clarified.

Alison regarded him. *Bolero's*. It had an upscale ring to it. "But . . . " She looked down at her jacket, her jeans, her wet and dirty shoes. "I'm not sure a place with the name Bolero's would allow me inside."

David laughed. "They would, but I have a suggestion. If you're not too starved by the time we get to Taos, we could stop at home and both change into something more appropriate. Bolero's serves dinner until midnight. And," he added, "I doubt we'll be fighting snow in Taos. It'll probably be sixty-five degrees with a light breeze and starlit skies."

Instantly, Alison felt on guard. But she couldn't think of an excuse. Not that she wanted to. Dinner at a fancy restaurant with David for company. A starlit sky and a light breeze. The prospect was far too enticing.

David turned from her to put the Jeep in gear. "Well, what do you say, Alison?"

"I'd love to go to dinner." There, she had said it and she couldn't take it back. As they set off in the swirling snow, the deepening dusk, Alison told herself that having a meal with David didn't qualify as a date.

She had happened to be along today because that was the arrangement they had made so that she could teach Miguel. Perhaps David felt guilty for inconveniencing her this afternoon, though the emergency with the mare and colt had been none of his fault. Or perhaps asking her to dinner was simply his way of showing his gratitude for her attention to Miguel or for her support and patience through the small crisis just past. In any case, it was a kind gesture on his part, much like José making her comfortable in his kitchen and giving her coffee. It had absolutely nothing to do with the kiss they had shared in the parlor. Nothing at all.

Chapter Nine

"You look pensive, Alison."

"Do I?" She took a sip of Chablis from the wineglass she held in her hand. Then she set the glass down beside her empty plate.

"Was your dinner all right?"

"Dinner was perfect, David." She looked at him across the table with its mauve linen tablecloth, its vase of pink and white roses and lighted candle floating in a crystal snifter. "Everything. The filet mignon and lobster tail, the wine, the atmosphere." *And the company too,* she might have told him, squirming a little under the heat of his gaze.

"I'm glad you like Bolero's." David lifted his wineglass to his lips and took a swallow.

Alison peered at him through lowered lashes. The twenty minutes or so they'd spent changing their clothes had wrought a sort of transformation in them both. In David's case, the result was not far short of spectacular.

As handsome as he was in a casual knit shirt and jeans,

Alison found him twice as appealing in his crisp white dress shirt and tan suede sport coat.

If she'd had any doubts as to her own choice of clothing for dinner, David had banished them. She had brought only three dresses with her and so her selection had been narrow. After a brief debate, she had chosen the peach silk dress with softly flared skirt that she'd bought just the month before.

The long look David had given her on first sight, his murmured words of appreciation, had caused her to blush and laugh self-consciously. She'd had to emphatically remind herself that their having dinner together was not a date.

But, as the evening progressed, it felt more and more like a date. And now, with their meal finished and only a little wine left in their goblets, Alison wondered if she had fooled herself about David's intentions—and her own.

In the plush, dusky atmosphere of Bolero's, it was hard to ignore his considerable charm. With his dark good looks enhanced by the play of candlelight across his features, Alison could imagine that he was as at home here as he was in the rustic atmosphere of Sheldon's Café, that he counted among his friends the movers and shakers of Taos as much as the unpretentious citizens of Valera.

"I wish I could read your mind just now."

David's quiet remark made Alison realize he'd known she was staring at him. She cast her eyes downward, perturbed at both herself and him. But she was determined not to let her irritation show. "I've . . . been thinking about today. I can't remember any time recently when I've enjoyed myself so much." That was true. She finally raised her eyes to meet David's. "I was thinking about the mare and foal, how glad I am that I saw the birth. I was thinking of Miguel, too, our lesson together. And I was thinking about José."

"José? Why José?" David pushed aside his plate and clasped his hands together on the table.

His curiosity encouraged her to express what had earlier crossed her mind. "His hospitality surprised me. He's such a humble man." She paused. "He's not married, is he?"

"No. Why?"

Did David think she was attracted to José? The idea was totally absurd, and David's expression told her that wasn't his concern. "Well, it occurred to me that it must be a rather lonely existence for him, living on his ranch by himself. Wouldn't you think so?"

David smiled. "If it were me, the answer would have to be yes."

His confession caused Alison to glance away again, but only for a moment. "I'd guess that most people wouldn't care for so much . . . aloneness."

David seemed to study the matter. "No, likely not. But, from what I can tell, José's pretty contented. Ranching is a hard way of life. Even considering it's a small spread, running the place all by himself keeps him busy most of the time. He might not be a bachelor forever, though."

"Oh?"

David grinned at her reaction. "He and Rosella have been, ah, dating for a couple of years now. Maybe not in the strictest sense of the word, but José almost never misses a dance at the community center. The dances are held once a month. The talk is that he and Rosella keep each other company, dancing the night away."

Alison tried to picture Rosella and José together. Since she didn't know either of them well, it was a bit difficult. But no doubt they made a good pair. "I hope it works out for them."

David didn't respond until he had drained the last of the Chablis from his goblet. "Yes, I do too," he said, but he seemed distracted.

Alison feared that she had inadvertently reminded him

of Eileen. Was he reminiscing about how it might have been if things had worked out for the two of them?

But then he smiled. "How about dessert? Bolero's serves a fantastic cheesecake. Authentic New York style, in case you're interested."

"It sounds tempting, but I'll have to pass. I couldn't eat another bite."

"In that case, I'll ask for our check when the waiter comes round again." David's hand came up to stifle a yawn.

All through dinner he had been animated, talkative. Alison had nearly forgotten he had worked all day. "You must be tired, David. I'll bet you'll sleep well tonight."

He shot her a rueful look. "Not for a while. I've got a paper that's calling for my attention as soon as I get home."

"A paper?" Was that the "paperwork" he'd once referred to?

"The subject, in layman's terms, is advances in the management and treatment of boils in goats."

"Really? You saw a pygmy goat with a boil just two weeks ago." She doubted she would ever forget their conversation in the Jeep just prior to the appointment. "Are you having the paper published in a journal?"

"It might be eventually. First, I have to present it at a veterinarians' conference that's coming up next week in Portland, Oregon."

"You'll be going to Portland next week?" For some odd reason the notion of David being gone so far from home bothered her a trifle.

"Uh-huh. I'm sort of looking forward to it. I've never been there, but I've heard Portland's beautiful."

"I wouldn't know. I haven't been there, either. But I'm sure it's a lovely city."

"I'll be gone for six days."

"Six days."

"Yes."

They regarded each other. The candle, in its snifter, sputtered and went out.

"That's a shame," David said, frowning. "I was enjoying the way your hair looked by candlelight, all fiery and golden, like a sunset before a storm."

The man's a poet, Alison thought inanely. "What can I say to such flattery?"

"It's not flattery, and I don't think any words are necessary, Alison."

And they weren't. She was sure her expression had already given her away. Seeking a distraction, she reached for her purse and busied herself searching its depths for a mint. She didn't find one.

Mercifully, the waiter came with their bill and took the credit card David held out. In a short while he returned with the credit slip for David to sign.

Without further conversation, David helped Alison with the shawl she'd brought along in case there was a chill in the late-night air. But the wrap wasn't needed. Outside Bolero's the air was calm and mild, considering a snowstorm raged in the mountains.

Despite the heavy traffic at that late hour, the trip across town was a breeze compared to the tortuous route down from José's ranch. There wasn't a snowflake in sight, only a clear sky and stars.

David pulled into the driveway of the old home. Before Alison could protest, he got out and walked her up to the door.

The outside lamp was on, no doubt a demonstration of Lucy's motherliness. David unlocked the front door and let it swing back on its hinges. The house was dark and quiet, the only illumination a tepid pool of light spilling in from the lamp.

Alison turned to David. She wanted to express her gratitude for the meal.

But he was ahead of her. He took both of her hands in his. "Thank you for having dinner with me, Alison."

"I should thank you, David. It was fun."

"Yes . . . " His eyes were focused on her lips.

A warning sounded in Alison's mind. She must not allow him to kiss her, must say a fast goodnight and leave him before her resolve crumbled. She kept gazing up at him instead.

His mouth came close to hers; he said her name. She smelled the musky scent of his cologne.

But he didn't kiss her—not in the way she had expected. His lips brushed hers in a feather stroke that still managed to send a quiver from her head to her toes.

"Goodnight," he whispered, switching on the stairwell light so that she could make her way safely up the steps. Then he left her.

Alison stood for a moment after he was gone, trying to sort out the confusion that made it hard to think. Why did David Grier have to have such an effect on her? It seemed all her level-headed reasoning, her determination to consider him nothing more than a friend, had fled along with her vow not to let his lips touch hers again.

The ancient house surrounded her with its familiar silence. The absence of any sound, even a whisper of wind from outside, soon made Alison's ears ring.

But she wasn't alone. Somewhere, Tom was asleep in his bedroom. Thinking of the older man made her wonder if David had called to let him know they wouldn't be home for dinner once more. If he hadn't, Tom probably had drawn his own conclusions and not worried unduly.

In a short time she had come to have tender feelings for Tom. Yet she was discomfited by his persistent belief that David was in need of a wife—and his apparent idea that Alison herself was the perfect candidate for the "position."

As she started up the stairs to the loft, Alison told herself that Tom's notions were just that. She was not David's match—nor ever would be. And she had no doubt that David held the exact same opinion on the matter.

The snowstorm in the mountains made headlines in the next day's paper. "How about this?" Tom said, handing the front section to Alison across the table. "Looks like you and David had a bit of snow on your hands yesterday."

Alison took the paper and read part of the article. It was reported that the mountains had received a record snowfall for early September. There was an accompanying color photo of a lone aspen tree standing bare and forlorn, its branches stripped of leaves.

Alison was reminded of the meadow and aspen trees where David had stopped for her to do a sketch. She handed the paper back to Tom, telling him about the beauty of the meadow and about the visit to José's ranch and the birth of the foal.

But as for the subject of dinner at Bolero's, she talked of it only in the most casual terms. Despite her prudence, the older man grinned and sent her a wink that made her squirm. In an attempt to turn the tables on him, she chided, "Tom, I never did get to hear the finish of the Trout Creek Pass saga, as David called it."

"You mean he didn't finish that story like I asked him to?" Tom looked shocked.

"No. But don't be too upset with him. He told me another story instead, one nearly as interesting as yours." Alison didn't say what the story was. "So that means I'm still dying of curiosity."

The older man chuckled. "I'll be, Alison." He pondered the matter for a moment. "I reckon you've suffered in suspense long enough."

Tom pushed his plate aside, having finished his meal. He rested his arms on the table and leaned toward her. "Well, Alison, you see, it was like this for me and Elizabeth . . . "

*   *   *

For the rest of the week, Alison spent most of her waking hours in her studio. She worked at her painting with a vengeance. She had no time to waste.

Apparently, David didn't either. She saw not even as much as a glimpse of him as the days stretched to Friday. Between his patients and his paper on boils, he must be fully occupied. The thought of him presenting his paper in a serious manner before a group of equally serious colleagues caused Alison to giggle. But the subject of the paper provoked images in her head of David and herself sitting in the Jeep after leaving Valera, of the way his quip about a boil had waylaid a kiss.

Despite the occasional wanderings of her mind, Alison still made considerable progress. She finished a watercolor scene of the meadow and trees and started two new paintings, one a gouache portrait of the mare and foal, the other, a watercolor of the Angel of Mora's grave.

On Saturday morning when she came down to her studio, she took inventory of her tubes of paints. She discovered the tube of Hunter green was nearly empty. A trip to the art supply store was in order.

To save time, she decided to take the Taurus instead of walking. And since she would be downtown, she might as well make a side trip to St. Ignacio's and do the tracing of the Angel's grave.

As she rolled up two pieces of tracing paper to fit in her knapsack, she permitted herself a glimpse out the window at David's *casa*. The place looked deserted. There was no sign of David or Huffy.

She knew David hadn't left for Portland yet. Tom had informed her that David would be catching a plane from Santa Fe on Sunday and would return the following Friday evening.

Well, it didn't matter when he went or came back. It was none of her affair. Grabbing her knapsack, she put the rolls of paper and her sketchbook in its pouch and headed out the door.

The same clerk at the art supply store greeted Alison in the same friendly manner as he had before. "You've come back for more supplies, I see."

She returned his smile. "Yes, but I nearly gave up on finding a parking place. There doesn't seem to be one within a mile of the plaza."

"There's a rodeo and fair going on this weekend."

That explained it. "Then I don't suppose that this would be a very good day to browse through Solaria."

The clerk looked chagrined. "If you would have come in two minutes sooner, I could have introduced you to the owner of Solaria. She was just here."

"Really?" Alison felt a stab of disappointment.

"Yes. Delphinia Rios stops in often. She's . . . "

But Alison heard no more. *Delphinia Rios.* The glamorous woman who had been the subject of Amelia and Esther's eager gossip was the owner of an art gallery. The finest in Taos, according to the clerk.

He was still chattering on. Alison came out of her state of surprise in time to hear him say " . . . and she's owned the gallery for just three years. What a turnaround for such a short period of time. It's almost a miracle."

"Yes. That's very interesting," Alison responded obliquely, hoping the man didn't notice her lapse in attention. "I'll be sure to visit Solaria soon."

He appeared satisfied with that. "You won't be sorry. Now how can I help you today?"

It didn't take long for Alison to make her purchase and be on her way to her next stop, St. Ignacio's. As she weaved through the traffic, her thoughts were preoccupied with the revelation that Delphinia Rios was the proprietor of an art gallery, not an actress or opera star as Alison had imagined she might be. Yet owning the finest gallery in

Taos was cause enough to make Ms. Rios a prominent figure in town. And being gorgeous besides certainly didn't hurt.

Within minutes, Alison came upon the graveyard. As on her first visit, the place looked deserted. She parked the Taurus at the curb and got out.

Knapsack slung over her shoulder, she walked the short distance to the wooden gate and let herself into the yard. She was glad to see the cemetery, shrouded in quiet dignity, was hers alone.

But she soon discovered that she wasn't the only one who'd come to St. Ignacio's recently. As she approached Rosa Chapman's grave, she caught a glint of something in a beam of sunlight. Kneeling down, she was amazed to find a spray of roses nestled in the grass at the base of Rosa's gravestone.

At first glimpse, she thought the flowers were made of silk. On closer examination, she saw there were beads of moisture on the fragile, partially opened blooms. The roses were very fresh. Alison reached out and picked up the bouquet. She brought it to her nose and inhaled. The flowers smelled faintly sweet.

Who could have left them? Why? There was no answer to the first question, but Alison quickly discovered the "why" when she looked at the epitaph. Rosa Chapman had died on September 12. She recalled reading that on her first visit. A glance at her watch revealed that this year the twelfth would come in just two days, on a Monday.

Logic told her that the bouquet had been left in commemoration of Rosa Chapman's death. *The Angel of Mora.* Someone in Taos had not forgotten the Angel; someone had chosen to honor her memory.

A gust of wind came suddenly from nowhere. It tore at the roses in Alison's hand. Gingerly, she placed the bouquet back in the exact spot that she had found it. Then she took one of the rolled-up sheets of paper from her knapsack and did a tracing of the tombstone. On the other sheet of paper she made another sketch, adding the detail of the roses.

Alison sat down by the grave and contemplated the mystery surrounding Rosa Chapman. It was true that David had revealed a little of the Angel's story. But Alison longed to know more. And if for some reason David wouldn't—or couldn't—satisfy her curiosity, she would search for someone who could.

Chapter Ten

O n Saturday evening Alison was working diligently on the meadow scene when a soft knock came at the studio door.

She froze, hand poised in mid brushstroke. "The door's open," she called, finishing the stroke before laying her brush aside.

The door opened and David stepped into the room. Alison's heart quickened as he came toward her.

"Hi," he said, halting beside her. He appeared relaxed, but the smile he gave her was tentative.

"Hi, David."

There was a long pause as they regarded each other uneasily. Alison's mouth had gone dry, but it seemed she wasn't the only one who'd become self-conscious.

David spoke first. "I see you're busy. I'll just take a couple of minutes of your time."

"No, I'm not really busy. Well . . . " She saw the skeptical expression on David's face as he eyed her paint-splattered smock. "I suppose I am . . . busy, but not . . . that busy." They both laughed at once and it served to dispel some of the hesitancy between them. "Tom said you're leaving for Portland tomorrow. Did you finish your paper?"

"Almost." David briefly rubbed his eyes. "I've got to polish it a bit."

Alison saw then how tired he looked. There were hollows under his eyes and his chin sported a definite five o'clock shadow. She rather liked it, though she wasn't fond of beards in general.

David turned to the easel and examined the meadow scene. "Very nice," he said, but offered no further comment.

"I should have it done by tomorrow night."

"That's good." David shifted his attention back to her. "Alison, I've got some news I wanted to share with you."

"What?"

"Rosella called me earlier. She said Marie had her baby this morning, a girl, and both are doing fine. You remember Marie?"

"Of course. That's wonderful news, David." Alison recalled the shy but friendly young woman. "Marie said that you had found a midwife for her. I could tell she was very apreciative of that."

David looked away. "Marie and her husband, Felix, are special to me. They were my first clients among the ranchers of the area. After they learned I was planning to regularly hold clinic in Valera, they recommended my services to everyone they knew."

"Obviously Marie and Felix think very highly of you." Her observation must have pleased David, for his gaze met hers. Neither spoke for a moment, but it appeared he was in no hurry to rush off. "Could you stay just a bit longer?"

"Of course."

Alison smiled at that. "There's something I want to

show you." She got her sketchbook and opened it to the drawing she had made that afternoon. Her heart beat faster again as she asked, "Do you recognize this, David?"

He stared at the drawing for what seemed a very long time. "The Angel of Mora's headstone," he said finally.

"I stopped by St. Ignacio's today to fill in a few details for a sketch I'd done earlier of the stone. I came across a particular detail that I hadn't expected." She waited for David's reaction.

"What was it?" he asked, though from his expression she doubted the question was necessary.

"The roses, of course. They were real; beads of water were still on the petals. The bouquet must have been left at the grave shortly before I got there. David . . . " She searched his face. "Monday will be the anniversary date of Rosa Chapman's death. The flowers can't be a coincidence. I believe they were put there in honor of her memory."

"I'm sure you're right."

"Tell me more about her. You can, can't you, David?" The moody darkening of his eyes revealed the truth.

Still, he hesitated. "I . . . "

"Please. Somehow I've gotten caught up in the Angel's story, and I won't be satisfied until I find out the whole truth about her."

David came closer. His hands took gentle hold of her shoulders. "And you think I can tell you the whole truth, Alison?"

"Yes, I do." A small tremor ran through her.

"You're right."

"When?" she whispered.

"How about when I get back from Portland?" he said just as softly.

"All right," she agreed.

David let his hands drop to his sides. "I should go now."

"Yes." Alison watched as he took a step away from her,

then another. "Enjoy your conference." His eyes stayed locked with hers. "And good luck with your paper."

"Thanks." He turned and walked out of the studio.

Alison regarded the sketch that she held in her hands. "So, what secrets would *you* tell me, Angel of Mora?" she asked aloud. But all she heard in reply was the sound of David's footsteps echoing down the empty hallway.

"What you need, Alison, is to get out of this house for a while."

Alison stared across the dinner table at Tom. "What makes you say that?"

"I don't mean to be a meddlesome old man." Tom stopped short. A smile lighted his creased face. "Well, sometimes I suppose I do. It's just I got the notion that a jaunt down some pretty country road might brighten you up."

Had she really been that glum? Alison considered his advice as she plucked a roll from the basket and tore off a small piece. She buttered the morsel and ate it before replying. "Maybe you're right, Tom."

"I am. You'll see. And in only a couple more days, David'll be back from his conference."

So that was why Tom believed she needed an outing. To take her mind off David. She wanted to reassure Tom that her recent moodiness had absolutely nothing to do with David's absence. But how could she hope to convince Tom of the fact when she wasn't sure herself?

She told herself she was crazy for missing David since she rarely saw him when he was in town. Yet the fact was she had been strangely listless in his absence—and lousy company for Tom at dinner.

There was a soft whimper from under the table where Huffy lay by Tom's feet.

"You miss David, too don't you, boy?" Tom asked.

Alison chose to ignore the comment. "You know, Tom,

I've wanted to visit the Taos Pueblo, but I haven't had the chance yet. I think I'll go there tomorrow.'' She had an idea. ''Would you like to come along?''

He held up his hand. ''I'd like to a lot, but I'm afraid I'll have to pass on it. Tomorrow's my bridge club meeting at the Senior Center. We old coyotes still enjoy getting together to see who's the wiliest.'' His eyes sparkled.

Alison could have told him who was the wiliest. ''Sounds like fun,'' she said, smiling. ''How about you, Huffy?'' There was no response.

''Looks as if you'll be on your own tomorrow,'' Tom said with a laugh.

The next morning dawned damp and cloudy. Alison stood on the balcony of the loft, peering up at the sky. From the appearance of it, another snowstorm could be brewing in the mountains.

After dressing warmly in jeans and a cable-knit sweater, Alison twisted her hair back into a sensible braid. Let a storm blow in, she thought with a smile. She would ask Lucy to make her a thermos of hot chocolate—and not scoff if the housekeeper warned her to take her jacket with her.

Taos Pueblo was located only a few miles outside of town, but like St. Ignacio's cemetery, the Indian dwelling seemed worlds away. Alison spent the entire morning there. Perhaps because of the weather, few tourists were about, and she was able to take her time sketching a few scenes to add to her growing collection.

As she sat at an unobtrusive distance drawing an elderly Indian woman at her pottery wheel, Alison recalled Elizabeth's embarrassing exit from the grounds. Over dinner she would have to tell Tom that nothing quite that exciting had happened to her.

By afternoon the wind had grown sharper, and Alison's

supply of hot chocolate was nearly depleted. She left the Pueblo behind to take one of those country roads that Tom had mentioned. Following the map she'd brought with her, she was cautious to avoid any routes that looked like they might lead too high into the mountains. Dark, heavy clouds already blanketed the peaks. She shuddered at the idea of getting caught in a storm when she was on her own.

Interestingly, she did see several stands of aspen trees. Their leaves had turned from green to gold just as David had described. Yet today Alison found their color less dazzling than she had expected. Was the trees' beauty tempered by the dreariness of the lowering sky? Or, Alison wondered, was there another reason for her lack of enthusiasm?

Whatever the truth, she didn't stop along the way to do any sketches. But her spirits lifted when she discovered the road she was on ended at the turnoff to Sheldon's Café. On impulse, she decided to stop in for a hamburger.

As soon as Alison came through the door of the restaurant, she saw Gracie. The teenager was slouched against the counter, looking bored. When she spotted Alison, she straightened. "Hey, Alison!" A grin spread across her face.

"Hi, Gracie."

The grin became a puzzled frown as the girl peered past Alison toward the door. "Okay, where is he?"

"Where's who?"

Gracie cracked her ever-present gum. "Come on," she said impatiently, craning her neck for a better peek.

"Oh, you mean David? He's not here."

Gracie scowled again. "I can see that. So what gives? You two have a fight or something?"

Alison shook her head. "No fight, Gracie. Didn't David tell you he'd be in Portland this week for a veterinarians' conference?"

"Dr. Dave never tells me anything important." She gave Alison a sly smile. "I'll bet you miss him, though."

Alison shrugged. "I suppose we all miss him, don't we?"

Gracie got the point. She turned away before Alison could tell if the girl was blushing. "You need a menu, Alison?"

"No. I know what I want."

Gracie led her to a booth on the opposite side of the café from where she and David had sat before. Two men sat at one of the other booths on that side, and a young couple with a child occupied another. A country-western ballad played over a loudspeaker in the room.

"What'll it be, Alison?" The teenager whipped out her order pad.

"A Mesquite Burger. No fries. And a glass of water."

The girl made a face. "No coffee or hot chocolate? In case you hadn't noticed, it's cold outside."

"As you see, I wore my jacket today. Lucy packed me a thermos of hot chocolate this morning and I drank every drop. It's a wonder I don't slosh when I walk."

Gracie giggled. "So it's just a burger and water then." She didn't move to leave, and Alison sensed the girl wanted to chat.

No doubt Gracie was eager to talk about David, but Alison wasn't inclined to accommodate her in that regard. There was a different subject, however, that might bear mentioning. "Gracie, can I ask you something?"

Gracie perked up. "Sure. And I'll bet I know what it is."

Alison didn't rise to the bait. She motioned for Gracie to come closer and, in a lowered voice, said, "Have you ever heard of the Angel of Mora?"

The girl's dark eyebrows arched. Obviously, it wasn't the question she'd expected. "The *who*?"

"The Angel of Mora." Alison strung out the words.

Gracie rolled her eyes upward; her jaw began to work

furiously on the gum in her mouth. Alison took it as a sign that Gracie was deep in thought.

"Angel of Mora," the girl repeated under her breath. Her brow furrowed. She chewed her gum some more, then pursed her lips. A pink bubble emerged; it grew until it burst with a loud pop.

Alison noted with amusement that the sound drew the attention of the other diners. The two men in their booth smiled indulgently. The child in the other booth broke into giggles.

But Gracie wouldn't have noticed. She was still contemplating. Finally she said, " 'Fraid you got me, Alison. I don't know any angels, but I'm curious about this one. The name sounds kind of, you know, *romantic*."

"You've never heard of her then?"

Gracie shrugged. "Nope. I guess angels aren't, uh, my thing exactly." The confident air, the impudent grin slipped back into place. "Tell you what, though. I have met a few . . . "

"Gracie! Order up!"

Gracie gasped; Alison stifled a cry of surprise. "Sorry, Alison. I . . . "

"Gotta go," Alison put in as Gracie hustled off.

"Hey," Gracie called over her shoulder, "I'll ask around about this Angel. And if I find out anything, you'll be the first to know. Okay?"

"Okay." Alison smiled at the teenager's retreating back. She could only imagine what it was that Gracie was about to confess when her father interrupted. Alison had to wonder, too, what the teenager would say if she learned that it was "Dr. Dave" who held the key to the Angel of Mora's secrets.

Chapter Eleven

On Thursday evening, Lucy told Alison and Tom that she would like to wait on dinner the next day until David got home. He was due back from his conference then, she said, and was scheduled to arrive home on the shuttle bus sometime between six and six-thirty.

"The bus is often late," she added, "but if you two wouldn't mind biding your time for a bit . . . "

"I think it's a fine idea," Tom interrupted, "and I can hold out a while for a meal and not be bothered. How about you, Alison?" He turned to her.

She felt his eyes on her, and Lucy's too. "Sure. I don't mind, either." She fidgeted briefly with her napkin, wondering if Lucy shared Tom's mistaken romantic notions about David and herself.

Lucy clasped her hands together in front of her. "Fine. It's all settled then. I'll roast a chicken and stuff it with corn-bread dressing. That's David's favorite," she confided to Alison. "And there'll be chocolate cake for dessert."

Tom chuckled. "A meal fit for royalty. My mouth's watering already."

"Just don't get too hungry," Lucy chided with a little smile. She gathered up several bowls and the roll basket from the table and left for the kitchen.

Alison peered across at Tom. "You know," he said to her, "this place isn't the same without David around. "It'll be good to have him back."

"Yes, of course." She hoped her answer didn't betray any undue enthusiasm on her part. But the truth was that she was only too eager for his return.

The next evening, Alison went down to the dining room just after six. She had put on a fresh pair of jeans and changed from her smock into a pink wool sweater. The weather had been blustery all day, more reminiscent of November than September, she thought.

Tom stood waiting for Alison by her chair. He helped her into it and sat down at his place. It was then Alison noticed the table was set with a festive-looking vase of yellow and white chrysanthemums and two lighted tapers.

"Lucy's done up the table real fancy tonight," Tom remarked with a grin.

"I see." Alison smiled over at him. She was about to say that the arrangement looked very pretty when Lucy appeared.

"David's on his way," the housekeeper announced.

Alison straightened; she checked her watch. It was just six-fifteen. For once the bus must have been on time.

David came through the door. He was wearing a tan trench coat and Alison thought that he looked very like a businessman who had just completed a successful junket. To her embarrassment, his eyes made instant contact with hers. He smiled as his gaze washed over her, and she was powerless to look away.

Alison's breath checked in her throat as her eyes stayed

locked with David's. Then David turned his attention toward Tom, and she found she could breathe again.

"Welcome home," Tom said.

David gave the older man a light thump on the arm. "Thanks, Tom. And thanks, Lucy, for holding dinner." He bestowed a quick kiss on the housekeeper's cheek.

Alison watched discreetly as David unbuttoned his coat and shrugged out of it. He draped it over a vacant chair. She saw that he wore a navy cable-knit sweater and jeans underneath.

"I'll get the food," Lucy murmured. She hustled off to the kitchen and returned bearing a huge tray laden with a steaming platter and bowls. David took the tray from her, holding it while she placed the various dishes of food on the table.

"The honor is yours," Tom said, gesturing to David.

David picked up the carving knife and fork that rested on the platter with the chicken. "Everybody ready?" He grinned at Alison, then proceeded to expertly carve the bird into pieces. Without asking, he reached for her plate. "White or dark meat, Alison?"

"White, please."

He placed two hearty slices of breast meat on her plate. "Tom?" He turned to the older man.

"My usual. A thigh and a drumstick."

Lucy stood and watched until David finished. "There's a special treat for Huffy in the kitchen," she told him and then left.

Alison regarded David curiously. "Huffy's having chicken, too?"

"You might say that. He gets the gizzard and liver."

"Mmm, tasty." She made a face and they all laughed.

As they feasted on the chicken and dressing, mashed potatoes, and glazed carrots that Lucy had prepared, Tom coaxed David to tell them about his conference. He did, peppering his account with numerous anecdotes. It seemed that a meeting of veterinarians was not the stuffy sort of affair Alison had imagined it to be.

By the time they finished their meal, conversation had dwindled and one of the tapers had lost its flame in a pool of melted wax.

Tom slumped back in his chair and patted his stomach. "Sorry to leave you two," he said, "but I've got a late engagement tonight." Not waiting for a response, he got up from the table and headed for the door.

Alison looked after Tom. "An engagement, that is, to play checkers with an old army buddy," David said, as if he'd heard her silent question.

"Are you sure?" She was only half teasing.

"About as sure as I am of anything with Tom." His expression turned serious. "I hope you don't have an engagement this evening, Alison."

After the briefest hesitation, she replied, "No."

"I'm glad, because I've missed sitting in the parlor and I'd enjoy some company. I'm sure Lucy's made a fire for us."

"It's cold outside, isn't it, David? Almost like winter."

"Winter's coming," he warned softly. "But remember what you said about a parlor?"

"It's a cozy place to be on a winter night."

"Or any dismal night." He got up, came around and pulled Alison's chair back for her. He reached for her hand and wrapped his fingers around hers. Then he led her down the hallway.

Lucy had laid a fire. Its cheery glow illuminated the center of the room, but left the corners in darkness. David let go of Alison's hand and went to switch on a lamp.

Alison sat down on one end of the sofa. David settled himself at the other end, turning sideways so that he faced her.

"You didn't tell us at dinner how your paper was received. I hope the presentation went well."

"It did, at least it seemed to from the comments I got afterwards. That was my first presentation at a big convention, so I had a pretty good case of nerves."

"I can imagine. I felt that way on my first day of teaching at the Institute. Actually, I felt on the verge of a breakdown the entire first semester."

David grinned. "I'm glad you survived so that now you can tell me what interesting things you did this week. That is, besides paint."

Alison shrugged. "Nothing earthshaking I'm afraid, though I did visit the Pueblo and took a short sight-seeing trip. Somehow I ended up at Sheldon's Café."

David draped his arm over the back of the sofa. "That could be interesting. How was Gracie?"

"She almost swallowed her gum when she saw that you weren't with me. She seemed crushed that you went away without letting her know."

"She'll get over the disappointment."

Alison smiled at him. "I suppose." She watched the fire for a moment. A log suddenly broke in two with a loud snap, surprising her. "I asked Gracie if she had ever heard of the Angel of Mora," she said at last.

"Had she?"

Alison met David's gaze. She thought that he looked vulnerable in the glow cast on his face by the fire. But she couldn't read his eyes. They were veiled in shadow. "Gracie declared that she didn't know any angels at all."

David gave a soft chuckle. "No, I wouldn't imagine that she does."

"But you do. Please tell me the rest of the Angel of Mora's story."

He responded by moving closer, though he didn't touch her or take her hand again. "I promised you that I would, didn't I, Alison?"

"I thought about her when I was at the Pueblo. Were Rosa and her parents Pueblo Indians?"

David shook his head. "The Novatos were of the Hopi tribe that inhabit the mesa lands of northern Arizona. Rosa's parents came to live in Mora before she was born, but they held on to their tribal heritage."

"You'd said that Rosa and Chapman had a baby. What happened to their child when they were . . . when Rosa died?"

"There was a kindly couple, neighbors of Rosa, who agreed to care for her baby daughter while she was gone." David regarded the fire; he seemed to find something of fascination in the bright blaze. Still staring at the flames, he went on, "It was the eleventh of September when Rosa left Mora alone on horseback. Her horse was as white as newly fallen snow, it is said, and Rosa's hair was as black as the midnight sky and so long that it reached the horse's flanks."

Alison shivered as her mind painted a mental image from David's words.

He continued, "In Taos lived a woman by the name of Maria Delgado. Rosa stayed with her while she inquired around town about Chapman. Someone told her that the bounty hunter was last seen heading north toward Cabrino Canyon."

"Cabrino Canyon?"

David nodded. "It's a box canyon not too far from Taos. The canyon's treacherous, with high cliffs on three sides. It's no place to be taken unawares by a storm."

"Is that where Rosa died?" Alison was sure of the answer before he gave it.

"Yes. She must have followed the trail that winds upward to the top of the west rim of the canyon. The weather changed suddenly that night. By the next day, the twelfth, there was a blizzard." David paused, then said softly, "A few days later, a rancher found Rosa's horse. It could barely walk. Its feet were frostbitten. But at least the animal survived."

"And Rosa didn't."

"When they heard the news, the townspeople of Mora mounted a search party. But the brutal weather forced them to turn back. The snow that had fallen stayed on the ground until spring, and that year the area had its worst winter on record. Rosa's body wasn't found until the next May."

Tears welled in Alison eyes. She turned from David to wipe them away. "How tragic." Her voice betrayed her emotions.

"Yes," David agreed quietly. He touched her arm. "There's something I need to show you, Alison. It's in my *casa*."

She looked back at him, puzzled.

But when he urged, "Come with me," she did, unprotesting.

They stopped at the dining room to retrieve David's coat. Instead of putting it on himself, he wrapped the coat snugly around Alison's shoulders. "To protect you from the wind," he said close to her ear. His hands lingered briefly on her arms. She thought she felt the light caress of his lips against her hair—or had she only imagined it?

They crossed the yard through the dark. David opened the door of his *casa*. He showed Alison inside, turning on an overhead light at the same time.

She was not surprised by what she saw. His small living room was furnished with a comfortable-looking sofa and chair. A couple of mountain scenes decorated one wall. A long, low bookcase crammed with books stood under the window. The room was tidy; there was no clutter. Alison found it altogether homey.

"Have a seat," David told her. "I'll be right back." He disappeared through a doorway.

Almost before Alison had settled herself in the chair, David returned bearing a large brown envelope in his hands. He gave the envelope to her. "Open it."

Alison did as he urged, reaching inside and pulling out

its contents. What she saw made her inhale sharply. "Oh, David." She held in her hands a photograph, a very old one, judging from its frayed edges and sepia tones.

It was a portrait of a young woman whose features bore the exotic beauty of an Indian princess. Cascades of black hair tumbled over her shoulders and down the bodice of her beaded, high-necked dress. Her eyes were dark, almost brooding, her mouth, full and sensual. Her face looked as though it had been chiseled by a sculptor who achieved perfection in his work.

Automatically, Alison's eyes were drawn to David. She studied his face. Should she have been shocked by what she saw there? For his features were a rougher, masculine copy of the young woman's in the photograph. "The Angel of Mora," she whispered, raising the picture so that it was level with David's face.

"Rosa Novato Chapman."

"And you, David?"

"I'm her great-grandson."

Her gaze stayed on his face a moment longer. "Yes, I see her in you." She lowered the photo to her lap and looked at it some more. "Why was she buried in Taos instead of Mora?"

"Her body was brought back here. Maria Delgado collected money for a headstone. She paid for Rosa's burial, too."

"What about Rosa's parents?"

"They had gone back to Arizona some time before and it was only after many months that they learned of their daughter's death." David sighed. "They never made the journey back to see her grave. Maybe they were too grieved. Or maybe they felt ashamed because they had disowned Rosa."

"And the baby?"

"The couple from Mora raised her."

"So your grandmother grew up in Mora."

David touched the photograph. He smiled. "No. Margarita Chapman grew up in Valera."

"Valera?" Alison couldn't hide her surprise.

"The couple, José and Sylvia Martinez, were originally from there. When my grandmother was three years old, they returned to Valera, where the couple lived until they died. José and Sylvia are buried in the old Valera cemetery."

Alison was beginning to see another dimension to David's interest in the villagers. "They must have relatives still living there."

"Miguel's uncle is their grandson. Rosella is their grand-niece. Most of the villagers are related, at least distantly."

"Is there any more to the Angel's story?"

"A little. A year after her burial, Maria visited the grave. She wasn't alone in the cemetery."

A shiver went up Alison's spine. "Who else was there?"

"A man. He had concealed himself behind a crypt, the one that still stands in the yard."

"The name Rodriguez is carved on it."

David nodded. "In broken English, the man begged Maria to tell him about the Angel."

"Did she?"

"Apparently moved by his plea, she told him. Afterward, she wrote in her diary that she believed the man was Chapman in disguise."

"If it was him, why wouldn't he want her to know? Wouldn't he have reclaimed his daughter?"

David's eyes clouded. "If it was Chapman, only he could have answered those questions," he said flatly.

Alison knew that David was right. She could also believe that if Chapman, by a miracle, had survived, he would have borne a terrible burden of guilt over Rosa's death. "The flowers I found by the stone—I'm certain Chapman didn't leave those. But you did, didn't you, David?"

"For years my grandmother would take roses to the grave on the anniversary of her mother's death. Two years ago, after I'd come back to Taos and shortly before her own death, she asked me to continue the tradition for her. I promised that I would."

Alison met David's eyes. "I sense you care very much about Rosa Chapman, even though you never knew her."

"It's true," he acknowledged. Taking the photograph from Alison's hands, he continued, "Perhaps the reason has to do with the legend itself, the feeling I get when I tell it. Or perhaps it's because I believe I'm like Rosa Chapman in certain ways."

He didn't elaborate on what he meant by that, nor did Alison ask him. But there was another question, one that was more important. "David, I wonder . . . I mean, would you mind if I borrowed this photograph for a short time? I'd like to see if I can do a portrait of her."

David didn't respond immediately, and Alison feared that she had been too bold. But when he took her hand in his, interlacing her fingers with his, she knew she needn't have worried. "Alison," he said, "I'd consider it an honor for you to paint the Angel of Mora."

Chapter Twelve

"**D**o you think Dr. Dave'll like my picture of Skeezer?"

"I think he'll love it." Alison grinned at Miguel.

The boy was holding the canvas carefully at arm's length as he walked beside Alison down the hallway of the community center. They had just finished their second lesson, and though the painting was only partially completed, Alison had agreed with Miguel that David and Rosella should see his progress on it. She was certain their comments would be of encouragement to him.

It was nearly noon now, according to Alison's watch. There would be just enough time for David to inspect the picture before Miguel had to go off to school.

When they reached the main room, Alison saw that David was finished with his patients. Well, almost. A tiny, frail-looking woman was trying to lead away a huge shaggy dog.

Alison and Miguel stopped to watch. The woman tugged

on the leash she had tied to the dog. The animal stubbornly resisted, bucking backward. In turn, she gave a sharp reprimand. That did no good, either. The dog merely sat down and refused to budge, despite the woman's mighty efforts.

"Uh-oh," Miguel said, "looks like Sam's making more trouble."

Alison took "Sam" to be the name of the hapless dog.

Just then David came along. The woman peered up at the veterinarian who towered over her in height.

After a word with her, David hoisted Sam into his arms and proceeded to carry him across the room to the front door of the center. The easy manner in which David handled the bulky dog reminded Alison of the way in which he'd bundled her case of supplies up the two flights of stairs to the loft and then back down to her new studio.

The task finished, David joined Alison and Miguel. "What do you have there, Miguel?"

"See! It's my picture of Skeezer." Miguel held the painting out for David's inspection. "It's not done yet."

David stared at the portrait for a moment. "This is turning out handsomely. "You're doing a great job, Miguel."

The youngster beamed. "Thanks, Dr. Dave."

Over Miguel's head, David said to Alison, "It's an excellent likeness of Skeezer. And I'd say you're an excellent instructor."

Alison wasn't sure who was more pleased by David's compliments—herself or Miguel.

"I got to go show my picture to Rosella," Miguel announced in exuberant fashion. "Bye, Miss Hughes. Bye, Dr. Dave," he called as he started off.

David chuckled, and Alison had to smile. The next thing she knew David had moved closer to her. She tensed at his nearness. "I can't remember when I've seen Miguel happier with something he's accomplished," David told her.

"I'm glad to hear that." Alison wished she didn't feel so warm—and wished she could say with certainty that

David wasn't the cause of it. But she also felt a sense of satisfaction mixed with frustration. "There's so little I can teach him in the short time I'm here. And so much I'd like to."

David faced her. "Alison, whatever he learns from you is a gift, an opportunity he wouldn't have otherwise had. Just remember that."

"I'll try."

He smiled at her. "And now, it's time we had our lunch. I'm hungry. How about you?"

David's afternoon rounds were finished quickly. There were just two scheduled appointments—one, to update a vaccination on a horse; the other, to check a leg wound on a calf. Neither took more than a few minutes.

Though there was snow on the ground that day, the roads were dry, the sky was blue, and the sun bright. The air had a briskness to it, but both Alison and David had come prepared with their jackets and boots.

It was a little after three when they headed back to Taos. David drove at a leisurely pace. When he passed the juncture near Sheldon's, for some reason he turned onto a narrow side road instead of staying on the main road.

Alison looked over at him. "Where are we going?" She wasn't alarmed, just curious.

"Cabrino Canyon." He threw her a glance. "That is, if you'd like to see the place now that you know the Angel's story."

Alison jumped at the chance. "I'd love to see the canyon."

Before long David steered the Jeep off the side road onto a dirt lane. Clean snow lay on the lane, unmarred by tire tracks. "It doesn't look like anyone's been here since the storm," Alison observed.

"No. Once the snows start, mainly hunters visit the canyon, and hare season doesn't start for a couple of weeks yet.''

Alison didn't ask, but she couldn't imagine that David would be one of those hunters.

David slowed the Jeep and brought it to a stop right in the middle of the lane. The two of them got out. Huffy soon followed, giving an excited *yip* as he jumped from the vehicle to the snowy ground. Immediately he took off at a run, kicking up little snow clouds as he went.

''Huffy seems to know the way.''

David smiled at Alison's remark. ''He does. We come up here sometimes in the summer. The canyon stays pretty quiet, even during the busiest part of the tourist season in Taos.''

''The kind of place to come to when you just want to be with your own thoughts.''

''Exactly, Alison.''

David reached for her hand and took it in his as they walked together up the lane. The mouth of the canyon wasn't far, perhaps several hundred yards. The entrance was narrow, but not claustrophobically so. There was adequate room for a horse and its rider to pass through, Alison surmised, remembering that Rosa had been on horseback.

In a moment she and David were on the other side, and she got her first glimpse of the canyon itself. She knew in that instant that nothing could have prepared her for the beauty that lay in front of her, that rose around and above her.

Her initial impression of Cabrino Canyon was of shadows and light and jagged rocks that rose to meet the sky. No sun shone here; it had already slipped out of sight behind one of the cliffs that surrounded the canyon on three sides.

But there was illumination coming from somewhere. Discovering its source, Alison knew she had been mistaken. A single shaft of sunlight had managed to reach the canyon floor from a crevice high up on the sheer wall.

As if by mutual consent, she and David came to a stop. He stood slightly behind her. Neither spoke for a time. There was no need, and Alison wasn't sure if she could find her voice just yet if she tried. It was enough to attempt to take in the majesty around her.

The colors were what captivated her most of all. Red sandstone cliffs backed by a deep sapphire blue sky. Bare, black cottonwoods set against a drape of virgin white snow. And there was a quietness here, unbroken by even the solitary cry of a bird. The only other sign of life, besides David and herself, was Huffy, and he had gone off on his own.

Alison became acutely aware of the canyon's isolation; that for all its grandeur, it could easily become a place of danger, a trap where even the most courageous of souls might be caught unaware by a sudden shift in the weather. The thought made her shiver.

At once, David's hands came up to rest on her shoulders. "Are you cold?" he asked, his breath a warm caress on her neck.

"No. It's not that, David. It's just that the canyon is so beautiful . . . and lonely."

"Yes," he agreed.

"Can you show me where . . . " She didn't have to finish the question. David turned her the other way so that she looked squarely in the direction of the line of sunlight.

"There. That's the west rim," he said.

Alison peered up at the imposing precipice and wondered how any living thing could climb its face of stone. She asked David.

"From here it looks impossible, Alison." His voice was low and very close to her ear. "But there's a trail that winds upward from the canyon floor to the top. An equally steep path winds down the other side."

Alison studied the west wall and saw—only in her mind, she knew, for anything else was impossible—an image of

Rosa Chapman there. The Angel of Mora looked just as David had described her, astride a horse the color of newly fallen snow, her long, raven hair tumbling clear to the animal's flanks.

"David, it's as if she . . . as if Rosa Chapman is up there now."

"I know," he said, taking her into his arms. "I've felt that way many times." He drew her close to himself.

David's nearness only served to sharpen the vision in Alison's mind. "But the Angel of Mora that I see isn't a woman who fears death, who knows she is about to die."

"You're right, Alison. Rosa Chapman holds her head high. She doesn't see the storm building. She doesn't feel the first cold flakes of snow fall on her cheeks."

David's whispered words echoed Alison's thoughts exactly. She turned so that she could see his expression. "That's how I'm going to remember the Angel of Mora," she said softly.

He framed her face in his hands, searched her eyes with his. "That's how you should remember her, Alison. And there's something else that I want you to remember." Lowering his mouth to hers, he kissed her.

It was not a kiss of friendship, but of far more, and she could not deny the fact. When they drew apart, she brought her hands up to rest possessively on David's jacket. Through the heavy material, his heart thudded beneath her touch.

His eyes, when she met them, reflected her own wonder. He started to speak. From out of nowhere a blast of wind came screeching down the canyon, tearing away David's words. The fierce gust tore at their clothes, lashed Alison's hair against her face.

Tenderly, David brushed back the strands and combed his fingers slowly through them. Then his lips took hers again and all Alison knew was the sweet warmth of his mouth on hers.

He released her at last, but kept one arm protectively about her waist. "We should go, Alison."

She heard him and realized that the wind had gone, the quiet returned to the canyon. "Yes, we should," she said.

David whistled twice for Huffy. The spaniel soon came on the run, tail wagging, to greet his master.

Alison took a last long look around her. She hadn't brought along her sketchbook, hadn't even considered it for some reason. Now she realized that she didn't need a drawing to remember what she had seen. The images, both real and imagined, were imprinted on her mind, heightened by David's kisses and the immediate disordering of her own emotions. No, she would not forget Cabrino Canyon or the Angel of Mora. She would not forget this day.

As they rode home, David seemed to withdraw into himself. Alison tried to respect his apparent wish for privacy. She told herself it was understandable. He had just revisited the place where his great-grandmother had lost her life. That would be enough to make anyone introspective. But was there another reason?

Huddled in the seat beside him, Alison grew restless as they traveled on and the silence continued. More questions crowded her mind. Was David feeling regret over the closeness they had shared in the canyon? Did he feel his behavior towards her had been inappropriate? Or her response to it? Or, like herself, was he attempting to sort through the twists and turns of their relationship, to define it in a way that he was comfortable with?

The label Alison came up with made her anything but comfortable. It was called *falling in love*, and it was the last thing in the world she had intended to do, and Taos, New Mexico, the last place on earth she would have believed it could happen. But it was happening—certainly to her—and for the moment she couldn't fight it. Maybe tomorrow her willpower would be intact again and she could order her life in a rational, sane way. She'd better, she told herself, for there was a load of painting to be done before she returned to the reality of Cincinnati and the Institute.

Finally they arrived home. David pulled into the driveway and brought the Jeep to a stop. "I'll walk you up," he said, glancing at Alison for the first time since they'd left Cabrino Canyon.

His voice sounded distant and formal. He gave her no chance to respond before he got out on his side and came around to meet her.

They walked briskly, heads bowed, hands in their jacket pockets, like two shy strangers. Huffy streaked past them, rounding the corner of the house.

At the front door, Alison gathered her courage and turned to face David. He looked past her.

Somehow she found her voice to speak. "Thank you for showing me Cabrino Canyon."

His eyes rose to meet hers, and she saw that a conflict brewed in them. "Alison . . . " He reached out to her, then withdrew his hand.

What was it he wanted to tell her? Could she help him? *Did she want to?* "Yes, David?"

I . . . What happened today, Alison, I realize now that I . . . we shouldn't . . . "

Alison stared at him in disbelief, barely comprehending what he was trying to say. She cut off his halting apology with, "Please, David. It's all right. You don't need to explain." She hadn't meant to sound icy, detached. But he had set the tone, and frustration boiled inside her. She felt humiliated.

She spun away from him and fumbled to unlatch the door, forgetting that it was locked. She found her key where she'd put it, deep in her jeans pocket. In her haste, she dropped it on the ground.

David scooped the key up before she could, got the door

open for her and gave her back the key. He didn't say anything, just let her go in and shut the door behind her.

Leaning against the wall, Alison struggled to make sense out of what had happened. It was impossible. All she could feel was anger—toward David, toward herself, too. From somewhere in the house came the faint sound of footsteps. Fearful they might be Tom's, she bolted up the stairs, taking them two at a time. It wasn't until she got to the loft that she realized the mad dash hadn't left her gasping for air.

The next day, winter came to Taos, or at least a foretaste of it. The morning had started off dreary, overcast, and cold. By noon, it had begun to snow.

The weather did nothing to lift Alison's already gloomy spirits. But there was work to be done. With a certain determination, she had dressed for the chill that permeated the house and gone down to her studio.

She got out her brushes and tubes of paint, took a board from the cabinet, tacked art paper to it, and placed it on her easel. Then she set Rosa Chapman's faded photograph on the counter and stared at it for quite some while.

Alison knew what kind of portrait she wanted to paint. Despite her sense of utter discontent the night before, when she had fallen asleep she had dreamed of Cabrino Canyon and the Angel of Mora. Now she recalled in her mind the images, both real and imagined.

At last she felt ready to begin. Taking her sketchbook in hand, she started to draw.

Hours and many discarded pages later, she had completed a preliminary drawing she was pleased with. She got up and stretched. To give her eyes a rest, she switched off the overhead bulb she'd had on all day and went over to the window. She noticed it had stopped snowing, but the sky was still banked with clouds.

She tried to avoid looking in the direction of David's

casa, but a beam of light caught her eye and she saw that it came from David's living room window. It spilled into the yard and illuminated the soft drifts of snow that had accumulated there.

David must be home early, she thought. She pictured him inside, lounging on the sofa, Huffy at his feet. The imagined scene stirred her emotions all over again.

Alison turned away from the view, determined to push the subject of David Grier out of her mind. But, as she snapped on the light and went back to her drawing of Rosa Chapman, she wondered how she could forget David when soon every brushstroke would rekindle a memory of him.

More than a week passed before Alison saw David again. She had spent most of her waking hours ensconced in her studio, alternately working on her portrait of the Angel of Mora and two Pueblo Indian scenes.

When there was a knock at her door on Tuesday evening, she gave a little jump, causing the brush in her hand to miss its intended mark on the canvas.

"Alison?"

"Just a second, David." There was a tremor in her voice that she couldn't help. Her thoughts raced ahead. Why had he come? What did he want? She laid her palette and brush aside, gained the presence of mind to turn her easel to the wall. Even if they weren't on the best of terms, she didn't want David to see her portrait of his great-grandmother until it was finished.

She went to the door and opened it to David. Against her will, Alison drank in the sight of him. He wore a tan camel hair coat and black leather gloves. Her nose detected the now familiar scent of his cologne.

She realized she looked terribly grubby by comparison. But then the last time she had seen him dressed up, she had been too. It had been the night they had gone to dinner. From all appearances, this evening he must be taking someone else to dinner. Alison wondered who the fortunate woman was.

"May I come in? I don't have long."

"Yes . . . of course."

Alison backed up as David stepped inside. He brushed past her and went to stand beside the counter. Looking around, he said, "You've been busy."

She didn't reply. There was no need. His attention returned to her, but she could read nothing from his expression. The only sign that he might be less than at ease was the slow flexing of his fingers in the gloves.

"I have something to tell you, Alison."

Her hands began to tremble. "What?"

"Yesterday I had lunch with the owner of one of the local galleries. Her name is Delphinia Rios and her gallery, Solaria, has the reputation of being the finest in Taos."

Lunch . . . with Delphinia Rios. The words hit Alison, and for a moment that was all she heard of David's conversation as she remembered the outdoor café and the gossip of the two elderly women seated at the table beside hers. Their talk had centered on Delphinia Rios. *"She's seeing a younger man,"* one of the women had said. *"Only in his twenties. And very handsome."*

"Alison?"

David spoke her name very softly. She peered up to find him standing in front of her. He was frowning. She felt compelled to say something. "I'm sorry. What were you telling me about Solaria . . . and Delphinia Rios?"

"As Delphinia and I were eating our lunch, she told me that in three weeks she'll be hosting an exhibit that will showcase the talent of up-and-coming artists. So naturally, I told her about you."

"You did?"

For an instant David looked amused. "Would you expect me not to mention you?" He turned away from her and went to lean against the counter. "I told her how good you are, how you had come to Taos on a grant. Delphinia was impressed. Alison . . . '' He paused, as if to make sure she was listening this time. ''Delphinia wants to meet you and see some of your work. If you agree, and she likes your paintings, you'll be invited to participate in the exhibit. It would be a great opportunity to advance your career,'' he added quietly.

What response could she give him? ''I don't know.''

''Say you'll at least show her a couple of paintings.''

Would he think she was crazy if she refused? She saw him check his watch and knew she had no time to debate the matter. ''Okay. I'll meet her. When?''

David smiled for the first time since their strained parting a week ago. ''How about tomorrow evening?''

Tension built inside her. ''All right.''

''Good. I'll plan to pick you up here around seven.''

Alison wanted to say that there was no need for him to come by for her. But she couldn't. All she could do was nod her agreement and watch as David went out the door.

Alone again with only her thoughts for company, she began to seriously wonder if David could be the ''younger man'' whose company Delphinia Rios enjoyed. If he was, Alison reasoned, that could explain his bumbled apology for what had happened between them in Cabrino Canyon. It would explain a lot of things.

Whatever the case, she was not in the mood to do any more painting, or even to clean up the studio. Instead, she stuck her brushes in a jar of fresh water and left the rest of the room as it was.

Alison found the hallway cast in shadow, except for the light from the foyer at the other end. Halfway down the corridor, she heard voices coming from the foyer—a man's and a woman's. The man was David. But who was the woman?

Drawn by an almost fateful curiosity, Alison crept closer until she could see the pair. David had his back to her, but the woman was facing the hallway. Alison recognized her immediately.

"Are you ready, Delphinia?" David asked.

Delphinia Rios gazed up at him. "Yes," she said.

Alison sagged against the wall. Even that one word sounded alluring coming from the gallery owner's lips. Still, Alison was compelled to watch as Delphinia put her arm through David's. David switched off the light and the couple went out the front door.

Alison stood where she was, unable to move. She fought to calm the sick, sinking feeling that invaded her stomach. But she couldn't deny what she had seen. It was true, then. David was the man Delphinia was involved with.

Had the gallery owner been waiting for David in the foyer? Or had she just come? Or had she and David been together before his visit to the studio? *Did it matter?*

Finally Alison found the strength to grope her way over to the stairs. But she didn't bother to turn on the light again. Just now the hot sting of her tears made her welcome the darkness.

Chapter Thirteen

Alison slept fitfully that night. She woke with a start several times, knowing that she had dreamed about David, though exactly what she had dreamed about him was unclear.

By the next evening when he came for her, she was pretty much a basket case. They talked little on the way to Solaria, and she couldn't gauge from his expression what he might be thinking. *Guarded* was the best word she could think of to describe both their moods.

Her first glimpse of the gallery was of an unpretentious adobe building with a green canopy awning. A gold embossed sign on the front read, simply, *Solaria*.

David found a parking place not far from the gallery. "Are you ready?" he asked, looking over at her for the first time in many minutes.

Alison managed a tight smile. "I think I am." She wished she could say the words with conviction.

"Let's go then."

She reached in the back of the Jeep for the portfolio case she'd bought just that morning. David came around to meet her and she went with him up the sidewalk to the entrance of Solaria.

Delphinia met them at the door. "David!" She held out her hands to David and he took them.

"Delphinia," he responded, bending to place a kiss on her cheek.

Alison watched numbly, imagining what kind of kiss he might have given the gallery owner if she hadn't been there.

"And you're Alison Hughes."

Putting on another insincere smile, she said, "Yes, and of course you're Ms. Rios."

The gallery owner laughed. "Delphinia, please." She gestured with one perfectly manicured hand. "Come in, Alison, and let's see the paintings you brought for me to look at."

As soon as she stepped inside, Alison was struck by the elegant, spacious atmosphere of Solaria. No cluttered feeling here. The place was pure class. *Like the woman who owned it. The woman David was in love with.*

Alison turned to Delphinia, avoiding any eye contact with David. "Your gallery is lovely."

Delphinia gave her a dazzling smile. "Thank you, Alison. We do our best."

Standing so close, Alison noted that Delphinia's hair and coloring were a perfect match to David's, and her appearance was that of a woman who exuded self-confidence, who knew exactly what she wanted out of life and how to get it.

Delphinia reached out to touch David's arm in a possessive way. "Why don't you give us half an hour or so?" Her fingers lightly caressed the sleeve of David's shirt.

"I'll go across the street for a cup of espresso," he offered, though he made no move to go.

Despite all of her good intentions and her considerable nervousness, Alison began to do a slow burn. She felt like saying to David what a terrible sacrifice it must be to leave Delphinia's side for even one minute.

"Now, if you'll come with me."

Alison realized that Delphinia was talking to her. Studiously ignoring David, she started after the gallery owner. A hand on her shoulder stopped her.

"Good luck, Alison."

She peered up to see David's face very near hers. "Thanks," she said curtly, then turned away.

Delphinia led her over to an easel that was set up near a display counter. "You can lay your portfolio there," she said. After Alison set her case down, Delphinia went on, "I understand you're an instructor at Glockner Art Institute. David tells me you've come to Taos on a grant."

"That's right."

"Excellent." Delphinia made a minor adjustment in the position of the easel. "Now why don't we start. If you'll display your first painting for me, please."

Alison opened the portfolio and took out the Pueblo scene. "I just completed this today, so it isn't quite dry yet."

"Oh, yes. The Taos Pueblo."

The tone of Delphinia's voice made Alison think the gallery owner had seen hundreds of similar paintings.

It was Delphinia's only remark. She motioned for Alison to take away the picture and set up the next one, which happened to be the mountain scene. Delphinia studied it for a moment, leaning close. She murmured something under her breath that Alison didn't catch. Then, with a wave of her hand, she dismissed that one too.

And so it went, through the portrait of Tom and Nubbins and a gouache rendering of the mare and foal. A queasy feeling took up residence in Alison's stomach.

"Is that all?" Delphinia regarded her with a slight frown.

Alison hesitated. "There's one more, but I brought only the pencil sketch. I'm working on the painting. It's nearly half finished." Her hands shook a little as she lifted out the drawing of Rosa Chapman.

The gallery owner retrieved a piece of board and several tacks. She took the sketch from Alison, secured it to the board with the tacks, and placed the board on the easel. Then she stood and stared at the drawing for a very long time. Or at least it seemed a long time to Alison. Finally she turned to Alison. "May I ask where you found the subject for this portrait?"

"From a very old photograph." Alison determined not to say any more. She was surprised that Delphinia apparently didn't know about the Angel of Mora. But no doubt that would change. As intimate as she and David were, he was bound to tell her the story one day.

Delphinia crossed her arms and gazed thoughtfully at the sketch. "Amazing." She shook her head. "Would you be able to finish the painting of the Indian Princess within three weeks?"

Alison's heart gave a sudden leap, yet she couldn't help smiling at the term Delphinia had used to describe Rosa Chapman. "Yes, I . . . I'm sure I could." *If I have to work day and night,* she vowed to herself.

"Wonderful! Then it will be ready in time for the show. I trust David's already told you all about the new artists exhibit."

Alison glanced away briefly. "He's told me some."

"Well, to fill you in, it will be held over the weekend of October seventh and eighth. I would prefer that you have at least three paintings in the show. The Indian Princess will be one of them, of course. You may select the others, but I particularly like the two portraits you brought today and the mountain village scene."

That meant she was in. Delphinia wanted her to be a part of the exhibit.

"I'm sure you're aware that whatever you enter in the show will be up for sale, with the gallery taking a percentage of the profits."

The piece of news took a moment to register. When it did, Alison's reaction was swift. "I'm sorry, Delphinia, but I'm . . ." Her mouth went dry. She started again. "I'm afraid I'm not prepared at present to sell the portrait of the Indian Princess."

Delphinia's face registered surprise; her voluptuous mouth turned down at the corners. "Are you certain?"

Alison felt weak. She was sure she'd just blown her chance to be in the exhibit. But selling the portrait was unthinkable. "Yes, I am. I plan to make the painting the centerpiece of a show I'll be participating in at the Institute next spring."

Delphinia gave her a sharp look, but said nothing for a moment. Then she offered a small smile. "I can see that you're determined on the matter. So the Indian Princess won't wear a price tag." She paused. "But I still want her on display. And I'd like to ask that you bring an additional painting or two that you wouldn't mind selling."

Alison had barely to consider the request before she said, "Yes, that'll be no problem." It was true she wouldn't have as many paintings to take back with her to Cincinnati. But there would be several weeks left after the show at Solaria before she was due to return home. And she had a healthy number of sketches to work with.

"Just one more thing. You'll need to deliver the paintings to the gallery on the Thursday afternoon before the exhibit."

"Fine. I'll remember that. And thank you, Delphinia."

"You're welcome." Delphinia went behind the counter and returned with a handful of small envelopes. She gave them to Alison. "Here are your invitations for the reception on Saturday night."

Alison opened the top envelope and took out the folded

piece of vellum paper that was inside. Embossed in silver, the invitation informed the recipient that he was cordially invited to a wine and cheese reception to help celebrate the new artists exhibit at Solaria Gallery. The reception was to be held on October 7 between the hours of seven and nine P.M. "I hadn't thought about a reception," she confessed, tucking the invitation back into its envelope.

Delphinia laughed. "Besides the wine and cheese, there'll be plenty of patrons eager to buy your paintings."

Alison wondered if that would really be the case, though the notion thrilled her. She wondered who she might invite. It was doubtful any of her colleagues could get away for the weekend. But there was Tom. And Rosella and Miguel. And Gracie. The idea of Gracie mingling with a crowd of art patrons made Alison smile.

"You'll be sure to give David one, won't you?"

The question brought Alison to immediate attention. Her puzzlement must have shown, because Delphinia laughed again.

"Of course, he'll be your escort, Alison."

Her escort?

At that instant there was a knock at the gallery door. "Ah, David's back." Delphinia sounded pleased. She went to let him in.

The pair spoke in low tones so that Alison didn't hear what they said. But she did hear their quiet laughter and her happiness was suddenly tainted. She also suspected the bit about David escorting her to opening night had been Delphinia's idea. Perhaps the gallery owner felt sorry for her and had sweetly persuaded David that the "budding artist" shouldn't have to make her entrance alone.

From under lowered lashes, Alison watched as Delphinia looped her arm through David's. Together, they made their way over to the counter.

"I believe congratulations are in order."

Alison looked up to find David standing in front of her.

His words sounded sincere, but his expression was guarded. She didn't have to ponder why. She also didn't want David to think, even for a second, that she was bothered by his involvement with Delphinia. She offered him what she hoped was a cheery smile. "Thank you, David. I couldn't be more excited."

It was clinic day and the weather had taken a pleasant turn from the unfavorable conditions of the week before.

But Alison's frame of mind was far from sunny. She told herself that her dark mood was caused by the pressure she felt in connection with her coming exhibit at Solaria. She had promised Delphinia that the portrait of the "Indian Princess" would be finished in time for the show and she meant to keep her promise. But it was putting her under a terrible strain.

Yet she was very much aware that her progress, or lack thereof, wasn't the sole cause of her glumness. As she'd feared, whenever she worked on the Angel's portrait, images of David intruded on her mind. And those images led invariably to other images. Of David and Delphinia in the hallway of the Ramirez home. Of David kissing Delphinia's cheek. Of Delphinia laying her hand possessively on his arm.

And now here she was with those images, seated beside David in the Jeep on their way to Valera. All because she had made another promise, one she couldn't bear to break.

Most of the trip was conducted in silence, giving Alison plenty of time to think. She considered the three invitations to the reception that she had brought with her. There was one for Miguel and his family and one for Rosella. And the third . . .

Glancing over at David, she felt discomfited all over again. She had put off telling him that he was expected to be her escort for the evening. Now, as he sat staring stonily ahead at the road, she debated how to approach him about the matter.

How had her life gotten so suddenly complicated? She sighed, falling back against the seat to watch the passing scenery without enthusiasm.

But, as they got closer to Valera, Alison began to see something that drew her immediate attention. What appeared to be thin wisps of smoke curled upward, marring the otherwise flawless sky. Something was wrong. "David! Look!" It was the first words either had spoken in miles. "Do you think there's a forest fire up ahead?"

Slowing the Jeep, David peered in the direction of the smoke. "I don't know. But we'll soon find out." He stepped on the gas again and the Jeep gunned down the road.

After they made the turnoff to Valera, it became obvious where the smoke was coming from. Alison's hands flew to her face. "No! The village is on fire!"

It seemed they couldn't get there fast enough. They finally came to a shuddering stop and Alison saw all too clearly what it was that had burned.

She and David jumped out of the Jeep at the same time and broke into a run toward what had once been the community center.

There was no recognizable building, just a smoldering heap of rubble and ashes. The acrid smell of smoke lay thick in the air; it burned Alison's lungs when she drew a deep breath. Around the perimeter of the ruins, people wandered aimlessly. Their faces wore the stunned expressions of those who have experienced some terrible trauma.

"I can't believe it, Alison."

She turned to look at David. The color was gone from his cheeks. "What could have happened to cause such a devastating fire?"

"I can't imagine, but the flames must have done their damage very quickly. There's nothing left—nothing."

"Dr. Dave! Miss Hughes!"

Alison saw Miguel hurrying their way as fast as his legs would allow.

"Miguel." David knelt down; Alison followed his lead. Miguel flung his frail arms around them both. He gazed up and Alison saw that his eyes were shiny with unshed tears.

"Do they know what caused the fire?" David asked quietly.

Miguel bowed his head. He swiped at his eyes with his hands. Alison sensed he was trying to be brave.

At that moment, Huffy came along. The spaniel nuzzled and licked Miguel's hand. The gesture seemed to comfort the boy so that he said at last, "It burned down. In the night. We were all asleep. 'Cept Carmen. She saw the fire first."

"And Carmen? Is she all right, Miguel?"

Miguel nodded. "She's staying at her sister's. But her house burned too."

David looked over Miguel at Alison. "Carmen's house is . . . was next to the community center."

Alison could only shake her head as she remembered the elderly woman she had met on her last visit. It was tragic enough that the people of Valera, who had so little to begin with, should lose the one building that had served many of their needs. The community's "heartbeat," David had called the center. But for Carmen Montez to lose her home . . .

"David!" a woman's voice called.

Alison looked around and saw that it was Rosella. She started to get up; David offered her his hand in assistance. Once she was standing, he still held onto her and a part of Alison was keenly aware of the determined way David's fingers interlaced with hers. She had no chance to debate the meaning of his actions. Rosella's obvious distress commanded her attention.

It was apparent Rosella had been crying. Her eyes were red and swollen. Her lips trembled as she tried to speak.

Alison put her free arm around Rosella's shoulder. "I'm very sorry," she whispered, though the words sounded woefully inadequate.

Rosella bowed her head. "It is . . . so sad."

David reached out to Rosella. "Does anyone have an idea what caused the fire?"

Rosella brought a tissue to her eyes and dabbed at them. She shook her head silently.

"Tell me what happened," he coaxed.

She sighed. "We were all asleep, the whole village. It was just after midnight when I heard a knock at my door. I know what hour it was because I looked at my clock and felt a little frightened that someone would want to get me out of bed." A ghost of a smile crossed Rosella's lips. "I went to the door and found Carmen standing there—in her nightgown."

"Go on," David urged.

"She was talking very fast. At first, I didn't understand what she was trying to tell me. She pulled me out the door of my house and pointed . . . and I saw the flames. I ran back inside and picked up the phone to call the Eagle Bend Fire Company." Her voice quavered. "The system was down. I couldn't call out."

Alison recalled what David had told her about the village's unreliable phone system. It had seemed humorous then.

Rosella continued, "By that time, others in the village had woken too. Everyone came out. We got hoses and buckets. Raúl went in his truck to Eagle Bend. But it was too late. The center . . . was gone."

"We'll rebuild. We have to." The terse words were David's.

Alison regarded him. His jaw was squarely set, his eyes hard and bright with sorrow and anger and a myriad of other emotions. And she understood why he felt as he did. In a very special way, he and the people of Valera were a part of each other. When they hurt, he did too.

Other villagers began to come forward. David excused himself from Alison and Rosella, saying he wanted to find Raul.

Alison watched as David threaded his way through the crowd, stopping often to talk or lay his hand on someone's shoulder. *They all look to him,* she thought. *They respect and trust his opinion.* And she had no doubt that he would more than help the villagers rebuild their center. He would be their rallying point.

Rosella tapped Alison's arm. "I must go too. Would you tell David something for me?"

"Of course."

"Let him know that he can hold clinic in my house today. And you and Miguel come and have your lesson there. That is, if it's possible to have a lesson under such circumstances."

Touched by Rosella's offer, Alison felt on the verge of tears herself. "That's kind of you, Rosella, but are you sure?"

"Very sure. There are still sick animals that need David's attention. And I know Miguel wants to show you what he's done on his painting."

Until that moment, Alison hadn't thought about Miguel's painting or the supplies she had given him. A sickening feeling filled her bones. "But wasn't the painting . . . everything destroyed in the fire?"

Rosella smiled, an oddly happy smile. "That is one good thing, Alison. Miguel was so anxious to practice that he took his easel and the painting and all his supplies home with him. I don't think any of it was lost."

Alison gripped Rosella's hand. "You can't imagine how glad I am to hear that."

Rosella gave Alison a hug. "Yes, I can," she said, then left.

Alison made a visual search of the area for David. She didn't see him, but was certain that he would return to her if she stayed put where she was. After a moment, she felt a tug on her coat. Looking around, she saw Miguel standing there. "I thought you had gone, Miguel."

"I did. But I came back." He shifted his gaze from her to an inspection of the ground in front of him. "I know who started the fire, Miss Hughes." He spoke with a quiet but bold determination.

Surprised by the revelation, Alison crouched down beside him. Finally, he lifted his eyes to meet hers. "*Who*, Miguel? You mean you think someone purposely set the center on fire?"

"Uh-huh." He shoved his hands in his ragged pants pocket. "It was Benny Benito from the village of Salas." Miguel's eyes narrowed. "Benny's mean. I heard him brag he was going to burn Joe Montano's barn last year. And then it burned down. But no one believed me when I said Benny did it."

"Miguel." Alison put her arm around his shoulder, drawing him near. His small body trembled and she wasn't sure whether it was anger or fear or merely a chill that caused it. She wondered why he had chosen to confide in her and whether he had again heard something that made him so certain of the fire's cause, or whether it was only a young boy's way of trying to comprehend the incomprehensible.

There was no chance to question him further. Alison saw that David was coming back to her. Miguel must have seen him too. He pulled away from Alison, hurriedly telling her, "I got to go and get my picture and stuff. See you at Rosella's."

Alison explained to David the arrangement to use Rosella's house for his clinic and Miguel's lesson. David said that, since Rosella lived nearby, they could walk and carry their things with them.

Miguel was already there when they got to Rosella's. So were a number of people with assorted animals in tow.

Somehow a semblance of order was established in the tiny home. David was given the dining alcove to use for the day's clinic. Alison and Miguel were offered a portion of the living room where there was a bit of space to set up the easel.

When Alison saw how much progress Miguel had made on the portrait of Skeezer, she was doubly grateful that the painting and Miguel's supplies had been spared from the fire. Though it wasn't easy, they worked at finishing it, and afterwards, Miguel was able to show it off to everyone who had gathered in the house.

"What would you like to start next?" Alison asked the boy when he returned. Miguel didn't think long. He brought out a drawing from the stack he always seemed to have with him. "This one," he said softly.

When Alison saw which it was, tears sprang in her eyes. "I think a painting of the community center would be a very fitting tribute, Miguel."

His smile reflected his sadness. "Dr. Dave says he'll help us get a new one."

Alison laid a hand on Miguel's shoulder. She saw implicit trust in the boy's eyes. "Yes, I'm sure he will, Miguel."

Somehow the morning passed and, despite his obvious reluctance to leave, David announced to Alison that they would still have to go on afternoon rounds.

Rosella insisted on providing lunch for the three of them, Miguel included. Suddenly, the meal became the perfect opportunity for Alison to hand out her invitations and tell Rosella and Miguel about the exhibit.

Rosella read hers. "I would very much like to come, Alison."

"Me, too," Miguel quickly put in.

Rosella reached over to tousle his hair. "Maybe we could go together, that is, maybe I could go along with you and your family."

He seemed to consider this. Then he frowned. "Probably they can't come." A small smile replaced the frown. "But I could go along with *you*."

"I hope all of you can come," Alison said and sincerely meant it. "José is welcome too," she added, then immediately wished she could take back her words.

Rosella cleared her throat, but said nothing.

Alison glanced at David; he looked slightly askance. Partly to cover her discomfort and partly because she saw no better time than the present, she said, "Here's yours, David."

"Mine?" he asked. His expression was concealed as he took the envelope from her.

Alison gave a little laugh to cover her sense of unease. "Of course. Delphinia said that you were to be my escort. In case you didn't know," she added with as much humor as she could muster. But she was sure she had failed to fool him.

David didn't laugh. "And is that what you want, for me to be your escort?"

He questioned her with such calmness, she wondered if Rosella and Miguel were fooled. But they—at least Rosella—must surely have noticed the sudden tension that filled the air. Alison's glance slid from one to the other and back to David. Regardless of what they might be thinking at that moment, regardless of her own shame, she knew she had to give David an answer.

"I believe it's what Delphinia expects, David, and that's what's important."

The words fell like heavy stones in the silence. In the next instant, David rose from his chair, muttering that it was past time for them to leave on their rounds.

"But . . . but you haven't had dessert yet," Rosella stammered.

"I don't want you to go! I don't want you to go!" Miguel cried in a sudden outburst of temper. Rosella hurried to the boy's side and put her arms around him.

Alison felt her face grow hot. For a moment she wished she could just crawl somewhere and die. Turning away, she told herself the problem was that they were all on edge, their nerves frayed by the tragedy of the fire. But, as she followed David from the dining room, she knew the feelings that lay simmering between the two of them ran far deeper than that.

Outside, a gust of wind hit Alison's cheeks, cooling the heat. Neither Rosella nor Miguel came after them, and she and David walked to the Jeep without speaking. David put his supplies in the boot. Then he whistled and called for Huffy, who must have been off exploring.

Alison threw her knapsack into the seat and was about to climb in herself when she saw Huffy racing towards them. The spaniel had something in his mouth. At first, Alison thought the object might be a small hare or ground mole. Huffy came to a stop in front of David and she saw that his "trophy" was only a tattered piece of cloth.

"What's this, boy?" David knelt beside Huffy and patted him on the head.

Curious, Alison bent down, grateful for the small diversion. On closer inspection, she noticed that the cloth bore a red-checkered print—and that its edges were blackened. "It looks like a handkerchief that got caught in the fire." She peeked at David to see his reaction.

"Maybe." He coaxed Huffy to part with the prize. "Or it might be a bandanna." He turned the piece of material over in his hands, then gave it to Alison.

She suspected that he, too, welcomed the opportunity to discuss something trivial. It would give them both time to compose themselves. But now the topic of conversation seemed nearly exhausted. "I think you're right, David. It is . . . was a bandanna." She was about to toss the cloth back to Huffy when she spotted what looked like an embroidered design in one corner. "What's this?" Smoothing the material over her palm, she saw the design clearly. Or rather, it was a set of initials.

Her heart gave a heavy thud as she made them out. "B.B.," she read aloud.

David came closer. "B.B.?"

Without thinking, Alison took hold of David's arm. "Benny Benito! This must belong to Benny Benito!"

David took the bandanna from her to inspect the initials. "How did you hear about Benny?" he asked.

"This morning Miguel confided in me." It gave her a certain satisfaction to say that. "He told me he knew who caused the fire, that it was Benny Benito."

"It's incredible, but . . . " David's eyes met hers. 'Miguel might be right. And this could be crucial evidence." He held up the singed bandanna.

For a moment, Alison felt a surge of triumph, of faith. "You said that Miguel was perceptive, wise beyond his years. And you're right, David." She grasped for confirmation of her hope. "I'm sure there was insurance on the center. Now the villagers can rebuild, and maybe Benny will confess . . . " She got no further.

"Insurance?" David cut in. He laughed bitterly. "Hardly anyone in Valera has insurance on his home, let alone the community center."

"No . . . insurance?" She didn't want to believe it, couldn't believe it. Yet she saw all around her the evidence of everything David had ever told her about Valera and its residents. Her hopes dimmed, her rekindled optimism flagged. Then she thought of David's promise to his friends. Somehow he would see to it that, like the legendary phoenix, a new community center would rise from the ashes of the old one. And for that, she admired him.

Chapter Fourteen

The seventh of October seemed to come all too quickly for Alison. She'd managed to complete the portrait of Rosa Chapman, but at the cost of several nights' sleep and a bad case of nerves.

Some of her worry, if not her fatigue, had been banished on Thursday when Delphinia had pronounced the portrait "magnificent." The gallery owner had even warned her, with a knowing smile, to be prepared to fend off at least one or two tempting bids on the painting.

But fending off tempting bids was not Alison's concern. Her mind was made up on the matter and no one, however eager and wealthy, could persuade her to part with her creation. What gnawed at her instead was the prospect of how David would react when he saw the portrait of his great-grandmother.

Since their fateful trip to Valera the day of the fire, she had seen David just once. He'd stopped by her studio with the news that Benny Benito had been arrested on suspicion of setting the fire. A confession was anticipated David had said, and that brought Alison a sense of relief, almost elation—until he cautioned her that even a conviction in the case would do nothing to aid the villagers in their struggle to build a new center. Benny Benito was poor too, and unemployed. The one consolation would be in knowing that justice was served.

The villagers' plight had affected Alison more deeply than she'd realized and she'd reasoned that her concern for them was the cause of her dejection.

But, by Saturday, Alison could no longer fool herself. As she began to prepare for the evening ahead, her mind was filled with thoughts of David and a sense of aching emptiness circled her heart and made her feel hollow inside.

She took a long, hot shower in hopes the hard pulse of the water would ease some of the soreness in her muscles. It did help, but she knew it wouldn't take much for the tension to return.

With a mighty effort, Alison made herself focus on the task at hand, which at the moment was applying her makeup. She took more care with it than usual, adding a bit of extra blush and eye shadow.

The job finished, she began to work on her hair. Her fingers moved nimbly, fashioning the long strands into a loose twist. She left a few tendrils to trail down the back of her neck and secured the rest with a carved ivory comb that she'd bought at a crafts fair last summer.

Alison turned to her closet and took down her plain black crepe dress. It had a high neckline and slim skirt. On the one occasion she'd worn it to an art show back home, she'd been told by several people that she looked very chic and sophisticated.

Not as chic or sophisticated as Delphinia Rios, I'll bet. "Stop it," Alison scolded herself aloud. Quickly, she slipped into the dress and did up the zipper in back.

She checked her watch; it was almost time to meet David. She gave her image in the mirror a last appraising look. There wasn't a glimmer of sophistication about her appearance that she could see. "You're being silly," she chided her reflection, then turned away.

Grabbing her shawl and beaded evening bag, Alison switched off the light in the loft and stepped into the hallway. She drew a deep breath and headed down the stairs. As she descended the last flight of steps, she caught sight of David coming in the front door.

He must have heard her high heels on the wooden steps, for he raised his head. "Hello, David." Did her voice sound as shaky as she suddenly felt?

"Hello, Alison." His eyes swept over her, then returned to linger on her face.

She gazed up at him, unable to look away. He wore his camel hair coat and stood straight, with his hands behind his back. The last time she had seen him in the coat, he had been on his way to Delphinia.

"I have something for you." He brought a gloved hand out from behind him. In it he held a large brown envelope, which he gave to her.

Surprised, Alison took it. She turned it over and saw her name written in a childish script. "This is from Miguel?" she guessed.

"Yes. I was in Valera a couple of days ago and he asked if I would give it to you. Just in case he couldn't come this evening, he said."

A stab of disappointment went through Alison, though all along she'd doubted the boy would be able to attend the opening. "So I won't get to see Miguel or Rosella then."

David shook his head. "Rosella called this morning to tell me there'd been another storm in the high country last night. The road out of Valera is closed."

"I'm sorry."

"They are too, Alison." David's eyes still held hers.

She felt a fresh sense of despair. This time, it was for

Miguel and Rosella and the whole village of Valera. They had just lost their community center. Now they had the prospect of a harsh winter ahead. "How are they . . . the villagers holding up?"

David shoved his hands in his coat pockets. "As well as they can under the circumstances. I've been in touch with a few people here in town. We're putting some wheels in motion to raise money for a new center." The hint of a confident smile crossed his lips. "We succeeded before. Why not again?"

At once Alison remembered the comment Rosella had made about David helping the villagers. She had been about to say more, then had seemed to abruptly change her mind. Now Alison suspected that Rosella had almost told her of David's fundraising efforts, but had thought better of it.

"Don't you want to take Miguel's present upstairs?"

The sound of David's voice brought Alison back. She studied the sealed envelope. On impulse she said, "I'd like to take it with me. Maybe I'll get a chance to open it at the gallery."

She was rewarded with a smile. "Why don't I hold onto it for you?" David offered. "I have an idea you'll be pretty well occupied the minute you set foot in Solaria."

"You wouldn't mind?"

His answer was to take the envelope and tuck it under his arm. "We'd better leave. Delphinia doesn't like to be kept waiting."

Alison averted her eyes, her satisfaction over Miguel's kind gesture suddenly dimmed by David's casual mention of the gallery owner's name and all that it implied. "No, I don't imagine that Delphinia does," she muttered under her breath.

David had been right. Almost the moment she stepped inside Solaria, Alison found herself being spirited away by

Delphinia. Her "escort" barely had time to offer to take her shawl for her.

Curiously, David received only the most cursory of greetings from Delphinia. *They're saving the hugs and kisses for later,* Alison thought grimly. Her one hope was that the happy couple would have the courtesy to restrain themselves until they were alone.

Still, Alison had to believe there would be a few compensations for herself this evening. To have her paintings hung in the most prestigious gallery in Taos should be reward enough, shouldn't it? Not long ago, it would have been. But tonight it wasn't and that troubled her far more than she wanted to admit.

"Don't you look stunning," Delphinia enthused, interrupting Alison's brooding thoughts.

The compliment sounded sincere, but while Alison smiled and voiced her gratitude, she knew it was actually Delphinia who was stunning. In contrast to her own choice of black, Delphinia was clad in white, from her intricately beaded clingy sweater and skirt to her elegant, high-heeled boots. The effect, with her dark hair and dramatic features, was both exotic and sensual. And there was the scent of some exquisitely feminine perfume that wafted from her.

Soon Alison realized that the scent was not entirely what Delphinia wore. As her gaze took in the room, her attention was drawn to the huge bouquets of tulips, roses, and varied wildflowers that were set about in clay pots and crystal vases. The sweet smell of spring lay gently on the air. "The flowers remind me of a country garden," she remarked to Delphinia.

"Glad you like it." Though Delphinia's reply was casual, there was a touch of pride in the words. "I'm sure you're dying to see what we did with your paintings. Then I'll take you around and introduce you to loads of important people, including your fellow artists."

Alison nodded. She wanted to meet the other artists,

though she was less eager to be introduced to "loads of important people." But she was especially anxious to see how her paintings were displayed—*The Angel of Mora*, in particular.

It was early yet, but Alison observed that the gallery was beginning to fill with people. All of the men and women that she passed were dressed to the nines and there was an unmistakable aura of wealth about the crowd. It was evident in the way they carried themselves, their very gestures.

"Ah, here we are," Delphinia announced.

They came to a stop in front of Alison's paintings. All she could do for a moment was stare. The presentation was beautiful, absolutely perfect. Should she have expected anything less from Delphinia Rios? But just what was it that made the mountain scene appear to glow? Or cause Tom to beam out at her from his portrait just as he did in real life? Or give the mare and foal a certain animated quality? Perhaps it was the lighting. Alison wasn't sure, but she loved the effect.

Yet it was Rosa Chapman's portrait that her gaze lingered on the longest. Delphinia had given the painting center stage in the display. Even to Alison's critical, subjective eye, the painting stood out as something special, projecting an ethereal radiance that befitted an Indian Princess.

Automatically, Alison cast an anxious eye around the room for David. There was no sign of him and she doubted he could have seen his great-grandmother's portrait yet.

"What do you think? Did we do a good job, Alison?"

Alison turned back to Delphinia in a sort of daze. "I'm . . . a little overwhelmed, truthfully," she confessed. "But extremely pleased with the way you've displayed my paintings."

"Wonderful! Then why don't we go on to the other exhibits?"

The next hour or so became something of a blur in Alison's mind. First, she was introduced to her fellow artists, two men and three women. They were every bit as talented as she'd expected them to be and she felt humbled once more to think that Delphinia had considered her paintings worthy of such company.

Waiters in black tuxedos moved deftly through the crowded room, bearing silver trays laden with champagne and plates of cheese and fancy breads and crackers. As one of them passed, Delphinia retrieved two flutes. She gave one to Alison. Taking a sip, Alison noted that the champagne was very dry and of exceptionally high quality.

When Delphinia seemed satisfied that Alison had met enough "important people," she left her at her own display to "receive all sorts of fantastic compliments."

There were compliments, some of them quite "fantastic," to Alison's surprise. Naturally, there were questions too. About where she was from. What brought her to Taos. Where her next exhibition would be staged.

Alison found herself repeating answers to the same questions as one group of patrons moved on to the next exhibit and another took its place. She imagined Delphinia making the rounds with each of the other artists in turn and then leaving them to their own devices. Well, it wasn't so bad, being the recipient of a hefty dose of praise.

But, as the evening progressed, Alison feared that none of her invited guests was going to show up, including Tom, whom she had counted on. She'd been less sure about Gracie. She had mailed Gracie's invitation to the café, hoping the incentive of getting to see "Dr. Dave" might be enough to entice the girl to come. But with the storm in the high country, even the roads nearer to Taos might be closed. And she had no idea where Gracie lived.

"Well, hello, young lady."

The familiar greeting instantly dispelled one of Alison's doubts. "Tom." She turned and watched the older man approach. He wore a gray suit that he didn't look entirely comfortable in. "What a wonderful surprise."

He cocked his head. "Surprise? Now Alison, you should have known I wouldn't miss your big night." His pleased expression turned into a frown as he gazed about the room. "Where is that fellow of yours? I haven't seen hide nor hair of him in days."

Alison's cheeks grew hot. "Come and see my paintings," she urged, taking hold of his arm to pull him along. She stopped in front of his portrait. "Look, Tom. You're a celebrity yourself tonight."

"I'll be! They hung my mug in a fancy place like this." He seemed wonder-struck—and for the moment drawn away from his quest to find David.

Before Alison could decide how to further distract Tom should he decide to query her about David again, her attention was diverted by someone calling her name. No, shrieking was a better word, she decided. But the voice was immediately recognizable. "Gracie." She turned around to greet the teenager.

It was Gracie, but her usual appearance was all but disguised by the florid makeup and tight red leather skirt and jacket that she wore. Huge hoop earrings completed the look of "sophistication" the girl was obviously striving to achieve.

Gracie grinned. "What do you think?" She seemed to have forgotten her gum, at least.

"You look very . . . grown-up," Alison said judiciously.

"Thanks." The girl gazed about her. "Wow! This place is radical, you know."

"I suppose it is." Alison rolled her eyes at Tom. He winked at her.

Gracie sauntered over to Tom's portrait. "Who's this handsome guy?" She flipped Tom a smile.

It hadn't occurred to Alison to introduce them. "Do you two know each other?"

" 'Course. We're buddies. Tom comes with David to the café, when you're not along."

Alison let the remark pass. "Are you addicted to Mesquite Burgers, Tom?"

"Nope. I crave the Elvis Burger."

She gave him a wan smile. "I see." Perhaps it wasn't that shocking. Tom was unique, one of a kind. So was the Elvis Burger.

"What's this?" Gracie tapped Alison's arm. She was staring, mouth open, at Rosa Chapman's portrait. "That's her! The angel you asked me about!"

Alison had to hide a smile.

"That's who?" Tom put in.

"*The Angel of Mora*," Gracie said importantly.

"An Indian Princess," Alison added, careful not to reveal any more. She perceived that Gracie was about to burst with curiosity.

Tom shook his head. It seemed that David had never shared the Angel's story with him. "She's a mighty beautiful woman, the way you've painted her, Alison."

"Thank you, Tom."

All at once, the older man grew alert. He gave Alison a nudge. "There's David now."

The words served to paralyze her for an instant. Then she saw that Tom was right. It was David and he was coming their way.

"Well, Gracie and I will be moving on."

Gracie took the hint. "Sure. That's cool, Tom, 'cause Alison and Dr. Dave got *things* to talk about."

Alison almost reached out to the pair, to tell them they were wrong about David and herself, that she and David had no "things" to talk about. But they hurried away and when she looked up, she found David at her side.

Chapter Fifteen

They regarded each other uneasily. David spoke first. "I thought you might like a glass of champagne." He offered her a flute. Then his gaze dropped to her hands. "But I see you already have one." He set the flute aside and gave her a tentative smile.

Alison lowered her eyes. "Thank you anyway, David." She took a sip of champagne from her half empty glass. The bubbles had gone out of it. "I guess I've had enough."

Surveying the room, she noted that the crowd was thinning out, and it seemed the chance had come for David to view the Angel's portrait. She cast about for something to bridge the awkward silence between them. "I was beginning to wonder if my escort had vanished."

"How could I vanish when I haven't seen your paintings yet? And when I promised to hold onto this for safekeeping." He produced the envelope from Miguel.

Alison took it. She'd found a brief diversion, a means of

putting David off for a moment. "This seems like a good time to open it, don't you think?"

"I would say as good a time as any." But then David turned his attention to her paintings and, from the expression on his face, Alison knew his gaze had fallen on *The Angel of Mora.*

Absently, she set Miguel's gift aside. Her eyes were glued on David as she waited in a sort of agony for his reaction. The longer she waited, the more anxious she grew, and the more loudly her heart pounded in her chest. She was amazed that David didn't hear it.

David's mouth turned down in a slight frown. What did it mean? Was he unhappy with her interpretation of the Angel's story? Did he feel she had taken too many liberties, let her imagination go too far when he'd been led to believe her intent was to do a simple portrait?

After what seemed an eternity, David looked at her, and Alison at once realized her fears were groundless, that she didn't need to hear any reassuring words from him, after all. The expression on his face spoke more eloquently than any verbal praise could have. "What can I say to you, Alison?" he said at last. There was a husky quality to his voice; his hands trembled when he raised them in a gesture. "How can I describe to you what I'm feeling right now?"

"You don't have to. I believe I know." To see him like that set Alison trembling too. And the pulse of her emotions beat so wildly at his nearness that she felt disoriented. She wanted to go to him, feel the sure strength of his arms drawing her into his embrace. She longed to hear his whispered words of love against her cheek, know again the sweetness of his kiss—and told herself that it was impossible.

Oblivious to her turmoil, David's attention was focused once more on the portrait. He touched its gilded frame. "This is exactly how I would paint the Angel, if I could," he said softly.

A lump rose in Alison's throat; she attempted to swallow it. "Don't you see, David. I couldn't have painted her that way if you hadn't shared her story with me. If you hadn't taken me to the place where her story ended."

As they stared at each other wordlessly, Alison wondered whether David was remembering other things about their visit to Cabrino Canyon. As on that day, she found herself drowning, helpless, in the dark depths of his eyes. The sound of a familiar voice calling her name jolted her back to reality. She turned and saw Delphinia.

The gallery owner wasn't alone. A man accompanied her. A very distinguished-looking man of indeterminate age, Alison observed. His hair was silver in color and very thick. He had a neatly trimmed mustache and his tanned face was youthful and smooth in appearance—like Delphinia's. Alison was sure she hadn't met him. She would have remembered someone that handsome.

That wasn't all. Delphinia and the man were standing very near each other and the man had his arm around Delphinia's waist. Alison's gaze shifted abruptly to David's face, looking for his reaction to the cozy scene.

To her shock, she saw that David was smiling. He extended a hand to the man. "Jonathan," he said, "good to see you."

"Good to see you too, David." Jonathan took David's hand and pumped it vigorously.

"Jonathan dear," Delphinia murmured, "I'd like to introduce you to Alison Hughes." She took hold of one of Alison's hands and squeezed it. "This is Jonathan Wright, and he'd like a word with you, if you don't mind."

Alison knew her confusion must show. She sought to cover it with a smile. "I'm pleased to meet you," she said to Jonathan Wright.

"The pleasure is mine, Alison." He nodded his head in a courtly manner before returning his attention to Delphinia. "I'll join you in a few minutes then?" His voice, in posing the question, was deep and intimate.

Delphinia tilted her head to gaze up at him. "Yes." The word sounded more like a breath, and the look on her face was one of pure adoration.

Alison gaped at them. She couldn't help herself. *Delphinia Rios is seeing a younger man. Only in his twenties. And very handsome.* The gossip came back to haunt her. She understood now that not a shred of it was true. If Delphinia was in love with anyone, it was with a distinctly *older* man by the name of Jonathan Wright.

"Why don't I take this for you?"

Alison became aware that David was speaking to her. "Your glass, Alison," he added with a puzzled expression.

He must consider her hopelessly dense. "Yes . . . all right," she stammered. As he reached out to take the flute from her hand, his fingers brushed against hers. This time, Alison chose to believe the contact was not accidental.

Then David and Delphinia left and Alison found herself alone with Jonathan Wright. "I was admiring your paintings earlier," he said. "Most of my collection is in watercolor. Still lifes. Pastoral scenes. Portraits." He gave Alison a thoughtful look. "Let me get right to the point. I would like to buy this painting." He indicated *The Angel of Mora*.

Alison's response was automatic. "I'm sorry, Mr. Wright, but that particular painting isn't for sale."

"Please. Call me Jonathan." He turned a charming smile on her. "Delphinia warned me that you weren't interested in selling. However, I thought perhaps I could persuade you to reconsider." He paused briefly. "I'm prepared to make you a very substantial offer." He told her how much.

The sum was so great that Alison wasn't sure she'd heard correctly. Then Jonathan repeated it and she knew there was no mistake. The figure danced through her head, threatening her composure.

For an anxious moment, Alison felt herself falter and she

had to fight off an unexpected temptation to say "yes" to Jonathan Wright. She'd thought her intention to hold onto the portrait was as good as written in stone. The idea that it might not be shamed her. Taking herself to task, she told Jonathan, "I'm flattered by your offer, but I'm afraid the answer is still no."

Jonathan shook his head. "Very well." He pulled a wallet out of his pants pocket and took a small card from it. He gave the card to Alison. "I'll be around for another half hour or so, should you change your mind. Or you can reach me at my office during the week. Call collect," he added with another gracious smile.

Alison looked at the card. It read, *Offices of Wright and Sanders, Attorneys at Law.* There was an address and phone number printed below the title. She wasn't surprised to learn that Jonathan Wright was an attorney. "Thank you, Jonathan," she said.

He raised a hand in acknowledgment.

Alison stood watching him as he strode off. Left on her own, she became aware that her knees were shaking. In fact, her whole body felt weak. She looked for a chair that she could collapse into for a few minutes. There was none to be found. Nor was there any sign of David or Delphinia.

Alison's gaze came back to the Angel's portrait and lingered there for a moment. As she turned away, she saw Miguel's envelope. She picked it up, looked again at her name written on the outside. She had meant to open the gift in David's presence, but perhaps it was just the sort of distraction that she needed now. On impulse, she pried loose the seal and emptied the envelope of its contents.

But what she saw dealt her composure another blow. Miguel's gift was a watercolor painting. Not just an ordinary painting, which would have been special enough, but a portrait of David holding his instrument case—and standing in front of the community center. Clipped to the portrait was a handwritten note.

As she read the note, tears welled uncontrollably in Alison's eyes. *Miguel has a perception of people that amazes me.* The full impact of David's words assailed Alison, causing her to perceive something too—a way in which she could help the villagers build a new community center. She had believed there was little she could do, besides offer comfort. Miguel's gift showed her that she'd been mistaken. But first she had to compose herself and then she had to find Jonathan Wright.

Alison discovered that he hadn't gone far. And he was alone. She seized the opportunity. "Jonathan."

His face registered surprise.

"I know this is unexpected, but I've decided to accept your offer on *The Angel of Mora.*"

Jonathan studied her closely for a moment. "Are you certain, Alison?"

"Very certain."

He shook his head. "I can't say I'm not a bit baffled." Then he smiled. "But I'm quite pleased as well. Would I be remiss if I asked what prompted such a sudden change of mind?"

She smiled too. "Not at all. I just realized that I have a very good use for the money. Though I can't say that I don't have any regrets over parting with the portrait. I had planned on featuring *The Angel* in an important show in Cincinnati next spring."

Jonathan's eyebrows rose. "Is that so? When exactly in the spring?"

She wondered why he would express such interest. No doubt it was because he was the epitome of a gentleman. "The first week of April. Actually, a colleague of mine is planning the exhibit. He invited me to display several of my paintings. It was to be a sort of coming out for me as an artist."

A smile lit Jonathan's face. "How very exciting for you. And what an incredible coincidence this is. There happens to be a Bar Association convention the very same week in Columbus. I'll be attending the convention, of course.'' He smiled at Alison. ''I believe we might be able to work out some sort of arrangement.''

''Arrangement?''

''Yes. More correctly, a loan. A loan from me to you of *The Angel of Mora*. I could bring the portrait with me so that you would have it for your exhibit. We can discuss the details later.''

''Wouldn't that be a terrible inconvenience for you?'' She prayed he wouldn't think so.

Jonathan shrugged, nonplussed. ''Perhaps a minor inconvenience. But one I'm willing to put up with. And this way we'll both be happy, won't we?''

His generosity had brought Alison close to tears again. For dignity's sake, she fought to contain them. ''Yes,'' she agreed, ''we'll both be happy.''

Jonathan accompanied her back to her display. He took a checkbook from an inner pocket of his suit jacket and made out a check. He explained to Alison that she should receive her money, minus the gallery's percentage, within a week. In turn, he would pick up the portrait from Solaria after the new artists exhibit was over.

He then wrote down her home phone number and address, promising to get in touch with her. They shook hands and he bid Alison good-bye and good wishes.

Alison stood, eyes closed, trying to absorb the fact that she'd really sold the painting. She didn't regret the decision; she couldn't. But she did wonder how she would tell David about it, though she had no doubt he would be pleased when she revealed what she meant to do with a portion of her earnings. And she would let him know that she intended to do another portrait of Rosa Chapman, one that would be for him.

She could see that familiar smile lighting his features, allowed herself to imagine him slipping an arm around her waist and drawing her close to whisper wonderful words in her ear. *Foolish dreamer,* she chided herself.

"Alison."

As if he'd broken into her thoughts, David was there. She mustered a smile as he came to stand beside her. Unable to hold back, she said, "I have some exciting news."

"Yes?" David looked down at her. His gaze roved slowly over her face.

"I just sold *The Angel of Mora* to Jonathan Wright."

His countenance swiftly changed. "You what?"

Unnerved by his response, Alison repeated what she'd just said.

David's eyes narrowed; his jaw hardened. "How could you do that?" he demanded.

Suddenly put on the defensive, Alison drew herself up to her full height. Yet he seemed to tower over her. "I'm sure I don't know what you mean, David."

He glowered at her. "I mean, how could you sell the portrait when you planned to feature it, center stage, in your exhibit back home?"

"And who told you what my plans were?"

"Delphinia, of course." David set his legs apart and crossed his arms. "I don't get it, Alison. She said you were so determined on the matter you were willing to risk being turned down for the new artists exhibit. And now . . . " His face flushed uncharacteristically. "Now you go accepting the first offer that comes your way."

Alison's cheeks burned from his rebuke. How could she ever have been so naive as to believe she loved this unreasonable man?

And did David imagine he had a claim on the painting because the subject was his great-grandmother? The question provoked a stab of guilt in Alison, but her anger overcame it. "If you would have given me one minute, David Grier, just one minute to explain instead of flying off on a tangent and accusing me of . . . of . . . '' She stopped, flustered. Just what was it he was accusing her of?

In exasperation, she picked up the portrait and note from Miguel and thrust them into David's hands. ''Here. Maybe this will help you to understand.''

He stared down at the portrait. Then his eyes met Alison's. She saw the look of anguish on his face and her anger dissolved. ''It's a very good likeness, don't you think, David?'' When he didn't respond, she urged, ''Why don't you read Miguel's note.''

David cleared his throat. He seemed to be struggling for composure. Then he began to read aloud, '' 'Dear Miss Hughes, I wanted you to have this painting of Dr. Dave and the community center. Pretty soon, you'll have to go home. I know you'll miss Dr. Dave just as much as he'll miss you.' '' His voice faltered and he paused. Finally, he went on, '' 'When you miss Dr. Dave too much, you can look at the painting and maybe you won't be so sad. I'm going to make one of you for Dr. Dave so that he won't be sad, either.' '' There was a postscript. '' 'Don't worry, Miss Hughes. We'll get a new community center. Dr. Dave said that we would.' ''

Alison reached out, took the portrait and note from David and laid them aside. She went to stand in front of *The Angel of Mora*. Her back to David, she said, ''I did refuse Jonathan's offer at first. But after I opened Miguel's gift, I realized that I had made a mistake. I knew there was a way I could help the people of Valera.'' She turned around to face David. ''And help you keep your word too.''

He smiled, but there was a look of profound respect in his eyes. ''Alison.'' Taking hold of her shoulders, he simply gazed at her.

Alison went on, ''Whatever I donate toward the new center isn't just my gift, David. It's Rosa Chapman's gift. And yours too. Don't you see?'' Her lower lip trembled and she was aware that the warmth from his hands was setting little fires under her skin, fires she had no wish to put out.

"Yes, I see," David said at last. "And there's something else I see." His hands slipped down from her shoulders to her arms, hovering there a moment. Then he took her firmly by the hand and led her away from the exhibit to a small alcove that was set in the wall. There, amid tall vases of wildflowers and potted plants, they were secluded from the sight of any patrons who might still be around.

The setting stirred Alison's memory, made her think briefly of the meadow where David had stopped that day so that she could make a sketch. But her attention soon returned to the present and the reality of David drawing her into his arms. It wasn't such a frivolous dream that she'd had, after all.

"I love you."

But this must be a dream, the words he'd just said. She could only stare up at him and wait for him to say them again.

He did—in a different sort of way. He lowered his mouth to hers and kissed her. The kiss was full of longing and sweet, silent promises. When it ended, they clung to each other for a moment. Then he told her, "I didn't want to fall in love with you, Alison. I knew you'd be in Taos just a short time and you made it pretty clear that your only interest was in your career."

"I guess I did do that, didn't I?" Strange how her perspective on things had changed. Her career was still vital to her, but she understood now that her painful breakup with Erik was responsible for many of her recent workaholic tendencies. She'd denied herself a life outside of the Institute. "I thought that . . . if I kept myself busy . . . concentrated on my career, I could be content."

"And are you . . . content?"

She squirmed a little. There he went, putting her on the

spot again. This time she knew it was deliberate. How could she answer him? "In . . . some ways I am, yes."

"But not in every way?" He didn't wait for a response from her. "Alison, I saw the hurt in your eyes when you told me about Erik. I knew that hurt because I've been there once too." His hold on her tightened. "But that was a long time ago. This is now. I've been ready to move on for some time. Are you?" he asked with more brutal frankness than usual.

"Yes," she said truthfully.

"Good. Because I need more than a picture of you to keep me from being sad, all due respect to Miguel." His hand came up to caress her cheek. "I need you," he whispered. "I want you with me . . . forever."

"Forever?" She turned her face so that she could place a kiss on the palm of his hand. He shuddered a little in response to her touch.

At last he said, "Could you live forever in the land of *Poco Tiempo*? Could you be content as the wife of an animal doctor who loves four-legged creatures and kids, not necessarily in that order?" He grinned, but doubt clouded his eyes.

A short time ago, the idea would have been absurd to her. Now it made perfect sense. She brought her face close to his. "Yes, on both counts." Drawing back slightly, she saw the doubt was gone; his eyes shone bright and clear again. "It's funny," she said, occupying her hands with straightening the crook that had somehow come into David's tie.

He watched her with fascination. "What is?"

"When I first came here, I thought what an unsuitable term *Land of Enchantment* was for a place full of sand and sagebrush. But now I know it's true." The tie back in place, Alison brought her arms up to circle David's neck. "There is a certain enchantment at work. At least in my case," she added with a smile.

David pulled her tightly against himself, his gaze focused on her lips. "Not just in your case," he said roughly. And, as if to prove the point, his mouth took hers in an appropriately enchanting kiss.